EGG MONSTERS FROM MARS

Look for more Goosebumps books
by R.L. Stine:
(see back of book for a complete listing)

Goosebumps®

EGG MONSTERS FROM MARS

R.L. STINE

AN
APPLE
PAPERBACK

SCHOLASTIC INC.
New York Toronto London Auckland Sydney

A PARACHUTE PRESS BOOK

ISBN 0-590-56879-5

12 11 10 9 8 7 6 5 4 3 2 1   6 7 8 9/9 0 1/0

Printed in the U.S.A.   40

First Scholastic printing, April 1996

My sister, Brandy, asked for an egg hunt for her tenth birthday party. And Brandy always gets what she wants.

She flashes her smile, the one that makes the dimples pop up in her cheeks. And she puts on her little baby face. Opens her green eyes wide and tugs at her curly red hair. "Please? Please? Can I have an egg hunt at my party?"

No way Mom and Dad can ever say no to her.

If Brandy asked for a red, white, and blue ostrich for her birthday, Dad would be out in the garage right now, painting an ostrich.

Brandy is good at getting her way. Real good. I'm her older brother, Dana Johnson. And I admit it. Even I have trouble saying no to Brandy.

I'm not little and cute like my sister. I have straight black hair that falls over my forehead. And I wear glasses. And I'm a little chubby. "Dana, don't look so serious." That's what Mom is always telling me.

"Dana has an old soul," Grandma Evelyn always says.

I don't really know what that means. I guess she means I'm more serious than most twelve-year-olds.

Maybe that's true. I'm not really serious all the time. I'm just curious about a lot of things. I'm very interested in science. I like studying bugs and plants and animals. I have an ant farm in my room. And two tarantulas.

And I have my own microscope. Last night I studied a toenail under the microscope. It was a lot more interesting than you might think.

I want to be a research scientist when I'm older. I'll have my own lab, and I'll study anything I want to.

Dad is a kind of chemist. He works for a perfume company. He mixes things together to make new smells. He calls them *fragrances*.

Before Mom met Dad, she worked in a lab. She did things with white rats.

So both of my parents are happy that I'm into science. They encourage me. But that doesn't mean they give me whatever I ask for.

If I asked Dad for a red, white, and blue ostrich for my birthday, do you know what he'd say? He'd say, "Go play with your sister's!"

Anyway, Brandy asked for an egg hunt for her birthday. Her birthday is a week before Easter, so it wasn't a crazy idea.

We have a very large backyard. It stretches all the way back to a small, trickling creek.

The yard is filled with bushes and trees and flower beds. And there's a big old doghouse, even though we don't have a dog.

Lots of good egg-hiding places.

So Brandy got her egg hunt. She invited her entire class.

You may not think that egg hunts are exciting. But Brandy's was.

Brandy's birthday came on a warm and sunny day. Only a few small cumulus clouds high in the sky. (I study clouds.)

Mom hurried out to the backyard after breakfast, lugging a big bucket of eggs. "I'll help you hide them," I told her.

"That wouldn't be fair, Dana," Mom replied. "You're going to be in the egg hunt too — remember?"

I almost forgot. Brandy usually doesn't want me hanging around when her friends come over. But today she said that I could be in the egg hunt. And so could my best friend, Anne Gravel.

Anne lives in the house next door. My mom is best friends with Anne's mom. Mrs. Gravel agreed to let Mom hide eggs all over their backyard too. So it's only fair that Anne gets to join in.

Anne is tall and skinny, and has long red-brown

hair. She's nearly a head taller than me. So every-one thinks she's older. But she's twelve too.

Anne is very funny. She's always cracking jokes. She makes fun of me because I'm so serious. But I don't mind. I know she's only joking.

That afternoon Anne and I stood on the drive-way and watched the kids from Brandy's class arrive at the party. Brandy handed each one of them a little straw basket.

They were really excited when Brandy told them about the egg hunt. And the girls got even more excited when Brandy told them the grand prize — one of those expensive American Girl dolls.

Of course the boys started to grumble. Brandy should have had a prize a boy might like. Some of the boys started using their baskets as Fris-bees. And others began wrestling in the grass.

"I was a lot more sophisticated when I was ten," I muttered to Anne.

"When you were ten, you liked Ninja Turtles," Anne replied, rolling her eyes.

"I did not!" I protested.

"Yes, you did," Anne insisted. "You wore a Ninja Turtle T-shirt to school every day."

I kicked some gravel across the driveway. "Just because I wore the shirt doesn't mean I liked them," I replied.

Anne flung back her long hair. She sneered at me. I hate it when Anne sneers at me. "You had

Ninja Turtle cups and plates at your tenth birthday party, Dana. And a Ninja Turtle tablecloth. And we played some kind of Ninja Turtle Pizza Pie-throwing game."

"But that doesn't mean I liked them!" I declared.

Three more girls from Brandy's class came running across the lawn. I recognized them. They were the girls I call the Hair Sisters. They're not sisters. But they spend all their time in Brandy's room after school doing each other's hair.

Dad moved slowly across the grass toward them. He had his camcorder up to his face. The three Hair Sisters waved to the camera and yelled, "Happy Birthday, Brandy!"

Dad tapes all our birthdays and vacations and big events. He keeps the tapes on a shelf in the den. We never watch them.

The sun beamed down. The grass smelled sweet and fresh. The spring leaves on the trees were just starting to unfurl.

"Okay — everyone follow me to the back!" Brandy ordered.

The kids lined up in twos and threes, carrying their baskets. Anne and I followed behind them. Dad walked backwards, busily taping everything.

Brandy led the way to the backyard. Mom was waiting there. "The eggs are hidden everywhere," Mom announced, sweeping her hand in the air. "Everywhere you can imagine."

"Okay, everyone!" Brandy cried. "At the count of three, the egg hunt begins! *One* — "

Anne leaned down and whispered in my ear. "Bet you five dollars I collect more eggs than you."

I smiled. Anne always knows how to make things more interesting.

"*Two* — "

"You've got a bet!" I told her.

"*Three!*" Brandy called.

The kids all cheered. The hunt for hidden eggs was on.

They all began hurrying through the backyard, bending down to pick up eggs. Some of them moved on hands and knees through the grass. Some worked in groups. Some searched through the yard on their own.

I turned and saw Anne stooping down, moving quickly along the side of the garage. She already had three eggs in her basket.

I can't let her win! I told myself. I sprang into action.

I ran past a cluster of girls around the old doghouse. And I kept moving.

I wanted to find an area of my own. A place where I could grab up a bunch of eggs without having to compete with the others.

I jogged across the tall grass, making my way to the back. I was all alone, nearly to the creek, when I started my search.

I spotted an egg hidden behind a small rock. I had to move fast. I wanted to win the bet.

I bent down, picked it up, and quickly dropped it into my basket.

Then I knelt down, set my basket on the ground, and started to search for more eggs.

But I jumped up when I heard a scream.

2

"Aaaaaiiiiii!"

The scream rang through the air.

I turned back toward the house. One of the Hair Sisters was waving her hand wildly, calling to the other girls. I grabbed up my basket and ran toward her.

"They're not hard-boiled!" I heard her cry as I came closer. And I saw the drippy yellow yolk running down the front of her white T-shirt.

"Mom didn't have time to hard-boil them," Brandy announced. "Or to paint them. I know it's weird. But there just wasn't time."

I raised my eyes to the house. Mom and Dad had both disappeared inside.

"Be careful," Brandy warned her party guests. "If you crack them — "

She didn't finish her sentence. I heard a wet *splat*.

Then laughter.

A boy had tossed an egg against the side of the doghouse.

"Cool!" one of the girls exclaimed.

Anne's big sheepdog, Stubby, came running out of the doghouse. I don't know why he likes to sleep in there. He's almost as big as the house.

But I didn't have time to think about Stubby.

Splat.

Another egg exploded, this time against the garage wall.

More laughter. Brandy's friends thought it was really hilarious.

"Egg fight! Egg fight!" two boys started to chant.

I ducked as an egg went sailing over my head. It landed with a *craaack* on the driveway.

Eggs were flying everywhere now. I stood there and gaped in amazement.

I heard a shrill shriek. I spun around to see that two of the Hair Sisters had runny yellow egg oozing in their hair. They were shouting and tugging at their hair and trying to pull the yellow gunk off with both hands.

Splat! Another egg hit the garage.

Craaack! Eggs bounced over the driveway.

I ducked down and searched for Anne. She probably went home, I figured. Anne enjoys a good laugh. But she's twelve, much too sophisticated for a babyish egg fight.

Well, when I'm wrong, I'm wrong.

"Think fast, Dana!" Anne screamed from behind me. I threw myself to the ground just in time. She heaved two eggs at once. They both whirred over my head and dropped onto the grass with a sickening *crack*.

"Stop it! Stop it!" I heard Brandy shrieking desperately. "It's my birthday! Stop it! It's my birthday!"

Thunk! Somebody hit Brandy in the chest with an egg.

Wild laughter rang out. Sticky yellow puddles covered the back lawn.

I raised my eyes to Anne. She was grinning back at me, about to let me have it again.

Time for action. I reached into my basket and pulled out the one and only egg I had picked up.

I raised it high above my head. Started to throw — but stopped.

The egg.

I lowered it and stared at it.

Stared hard at it.

Something was wrong with the egg.

Something was terribly wrong.

Briant

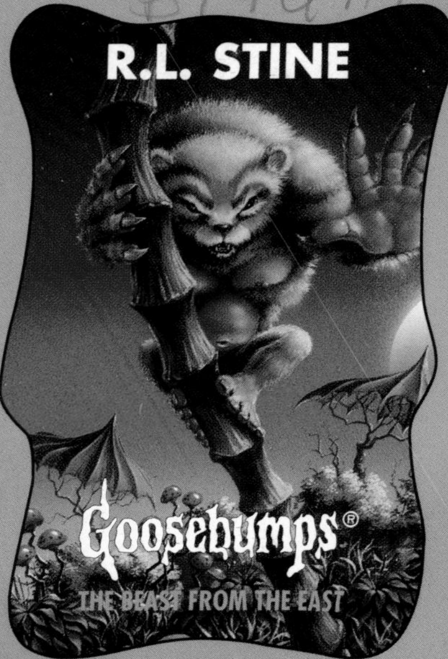

#43

STARRING:

GINGER WALD — Our narrator. She's the "sensible one."
NAT & PAT WALD — Ginger's identical twin brothers. No one
can tell them apart. They're twin terrors!
THE BEAST — He's a <u>real</u> animal!

SETTING:

A strange part of the woods. With yellow grass and
purple plants. It's out of this world.

SAY WHAT?!:

"Rule Zee — You must be three feet tall to play."

THE REAL DEAL:

"*THE BEAST FROM THE EAST* is based on a real hide-and-
seek game we played when we were kids. In our game,
no one was 'It.' We all just hid until it was time to go
home. It was kinda boring." — R.L. Stine

3

The egg was too big. Bigger than a normal egg. About the size of a softball.

I held it carefully, studying it. The color wasn't right either. It wasn't egg-colored. That creamy off-white. And it wasn't brown.

The egg was pale green. I raised it to the sunlight to make sure I was seeing correctly.

Yes. Green.

And what were those thick cracks up and down the shell?

I ran my pointer finger over the dark, jagged lines.

No. Not cracks. Some kind of veins. Blue-and-purple veins crisscrossing the green eggshell.

"Weird!" I muttered out loud.

Brandy's friends were shouting and shrieking. Eggs were flying all around me. An egg splattered over my sneakers. The yellow yolk oozed over my laces.

But I didn't care.

I rolled the strange egg over and over slowly between my hands. I brought it close to my face and squinted hard at the blue-and-purple veins.

"Ooh." I let out a low cry when I felt it pulsing.

The veins throbbed. I could feel a steady beat. *Thud. Thud. Thud.*

"Oh wow. *It's alive!*" I cried.

What had I found? It was totally weird. I couldn't wait to get it to my worktable and examine it.

But first I had to show it to Anne.

"Anne! Hey — Anne!" I called and started jogging toward her, holding the egg high in both hands.

I was staring at the egg. So I didn't see Stubby, her big sheepdog, run in front of me.

"Whooooa!"

I let out a cry as I fell over the dog.

And landed with a sickening crunch on top of my egg.

4

I jumped up quickly. Stubby started to lick my face. That dog has the *worst* breath!

I shoved him away and bent down to examine my egg.

"Hey!" I cried out in amazement. The egg wasn't broken. I picked it up carefully and rolled it in my hands.

Not a crack.

What a tough shell! I thought. My chest had landed on top of the egg. Pushed it into the ground. But the shell hadn't broken.

I wrapped my hands around the big egg as if soothing it.

I could feel the blue-and-purple veins pulsing.

Is something inside getting ready to hatch? I wondered. What kind of bird was inside it? Not a chicken, I knew. This was definitely not a hen's egg.

Splat!

Another egg smacked the side of the garage.

Kids were wrestling in the runny puddles of yolk on the grass. I turned in time to see a boy crack an egg over another boy's head.

"Stop it! Stop it!"

Brandy was screaming at the top of her lungs, trying to stop the egg fight before every single egg was smashed. I turned and saw Mom and Dad running across the yard.

"Hey, Anne — !" I called. I climbed to my feet, holding the weird egg carefully. Anne was frantically tossing eggs at three girls. The girls were bombarding her. Three to one — but Anne wasn't retreating.

"Anne — check this out!" I called, hurrying over to her. "You won't believe this egg!"

I stepped up beside her and held the egg out to her.

"No! Wait — !" I cried.

Too late.

Anne grabbed my egg and heaved it at the three girls.

5

"No — stop!" I wailed.

As I stared in horror, one of the three girls caught the egg in midair — and tossed it back.

I dove for it, making a headfirst slide. And grabbed the egg in one hand before it hit the gravel.

Was it broken?

No.

This shell must be made of steel! I told myself. I pulled myself to my feet, gripping the egg carefully. To my surprise, it felt hot. Burning hot.

"Whoa!" I nearly dropped it.

Throb. Throb. Throb.

It pulsed rapidly. I could feel the veins beating against my fingers.

I wanted to show the egg to Mom and Dad. But they were busy breaking up the egg fight.

Dad's face was bright red. He was shouting at Brandy and pointing to the yellow stains up and down the side of the garage.

Mom was trying to calm down two girls who were crying. They had egg yolk stuck to their hair and all over their clothes. They even had it stuck to their eyebrows. I guess that's why they were crying.

Behind them Stubby was having a feast. He was running around in circles, lapping up egg after egg from the grass, his bushy tail wagging like crazy.

What a party!

I decided to take my weird egg inside. I wanted to study it later. Maybe I'd break off a tiny piece of shell and look at it under the microscope. Then I'd make a tiny hole in the shell and try to see inside.

Throb. Throb.

The veins pounded against my hand. The egg still felt hot.

It might be a turtle egg, I decided. I walked carefully to the house, cradling it in both hands.

One morning last fall, Anne found a big box turtle on the curb in front of her house. She carried it into her backyard and called me over. She knew I'd want to study it.

It was a pretty big turtle. About the size of a lunch box. Anne and I wondered how it got to her curb.

Up in my room I had a book about turtles. I knew the book would help me identify it. I had hurried home to get the book. But Mom wouldn't let me go back out. I had to stay inside and have lunch.

When I got back to Anne's backyard, the turtle had vanished. I guess it wandered away.

Turtles can be pretty fast when they want to be.

As I carried my treasure into the house, I thought it might be a turtle egg. But why was it so hot? And why did it have those yucky veins all over it?

Eggs don't have veins — do they?

I hid the egg in my dresser drawer. I surrounded it with my balled-up socks to protect it. Then I closed the drawer slowly, carefully, and returned to the backyard.

Brandy's guests were all leaving as I stepped outside. They were covered in sticky eggs. They didn't look too happy.

Brandy didn't look too happy, either. Dad was busy shouting at her, angrily waving his arms, pointing to the gloppy egg stains all over the lawn.

"Why did you let this happen?" he screamed at her. "Why didn't you stop it?"

"I tried!" Brandy wailed. "I tried to stop it!"

"We'll have to have the garage painted," Mom murmured, shaking her head. "How will we ever mow the lawn?"

"This was the worst party I ever had!" Brandy

cried. She bent down and pulled chunks of egg-shell from her sneaker laces. Then she glared up at Mom. "It's all *your* fault!"

"Huh?" Mom gasped. "My fault?"

"You didn't hard-boil the eggs," Brandy accused. "So it's all your fault."

Mom started to protest — but bit her lip instead.

Brandy stood up and tossed the bits of eggshell to the ground. She flashed Mom her best dimpled smile. "Next year for my birthday, can we have a Make Your Own Ice-Cream Sundae party?"

That evening I wanted to study my weird green egg. But we had to go visit Grandma Evelyn and Grandpa Harry and take them out to dinner. They always make a big fuss about Brandy's birthday.

First, Brandy had to open her presents. Grandma Evelyn bought her a pair of pink fuzzy slippers that Brandy will never wear. She'll probably give them to Stubby as chew toys.

Brandy opened the biggest box next. She pulled out a pair of pink-and-white pajamas. Brandy made a big fuss about them and said she really needed pajamas. She did a pretty good acting job.

But how excited can you get over pajamas?

Her last present was a twenty-five-dollar gift certificate to the CD store at the mall. Nice present. "I'll go with you to make sure you don't pick out anything lame," I offered.

Brandy pretended she didn't hear me.

She gave our grandparents big hugs. Brandy is a big hugger. Then we all went out for dinner at the new Italian restaurant on the corner.

What did we talk about at dinner? Brandy's wild birthday party. When we told Grandma and Grandpa about the egg fight, they laughed and laughed.

It wasn't so funny in the afternoon. But a few hours later at dinner, we all had to admit it was pretty funny. Even Dad managed a smile or two.

I kept thinking about the egg in my dresser drawer. When we got back home, would I find a baby turtle on my socks?

Dinner stretched on and on. Grandpa Harry told all of his funny golfing stories. He tells them every time we visit. We always laugh anyway.

We didn't return home till really late. Brandy fell asleep in the car. And I could barely keep my eyes open.

I slunk up to my room and changed into pajamas. Then, with a loud yawn, I turned off the light. I knew I'd fall asleep the moment my head hit the pillow.

I fluffed my pillow the way I liked it. Then I slid into bed and pulled the quilt up to my chin.

I started to settle my head on the pillow when I heard the sound.

Thump. Thump. Thump.

Steady like a heartbeat. Only louder.

Much louder.

THUMP. THUMP. THUMP.

So loud, I could hear the dresser drawers rattling.

I sat straight up. Wide awake now. I stared through the darkness to my dresser.

THUMP. THUMP. THUMP.

I turned and lowered my feet to the floor.

Should I open the dresser drawer?

I sat in the darkness, trembling with excitement. With fear.

Listening to the steady thud.

Should I open the drawer and check it out?

Or should I run as far away as I could?

Thump, thump, THUMP.

I had to see what was happening in my dresser drawer.

Had the egg hatched? Was the turtle bumping up against the sides of the drawer, trying to climb out?

Was it a turtle?

Or was it something weird?

Suddenly I felt very afraid of it.

I took a deep breath and rose to my feet. My legs felt rubbery and weak as I made my way across the room. My mouth was suddenly as dry as cotton.

Thump, THUMP, thump.

I clicked on the light. Blinked several times, struggling to force my eyes to focus.

The steady thuds grew louder as I approached the dresser.

Heartbeats, I told myself.

Heartbeats of the creature inside the egg.

I grabbed the drawer handles with both hands. Took another deep breath.

Dana, this is your last chance to run away, I warned myself.

This is your last chance to leave the drawer safely closed.

Thump, thump, thump, thump, thump.

I tugged open the drawer and peered inside.

I stared in, amazed that nothing had changed. The egg sat exactly where I had left it. The blue-and-purple veins along the shell pulsed as before.

Feeling a little calmer, I picked it up.

"Ouch!"

I nearly dropped it. The shell was burning hot.

I cupped it in my hands and blew on it. "This is so totally weird," I murmured to myself.

Mom and Dad have to see it, I decided. Right now. Maybe they can tell me what it is.

They were still awake. I could hear them talking in their room down the hall.

I carried the egg carefully, cradling it in both hands. I had to knock on their door with my elbow. "It's me," I said.

"Dana, what is it?" Dad demanded grumpily. "It's been a long day. We're all very tired."

I pushed open their door a crack. "I have an egg I want to show you," I started.

"No eggs!" they both cried at once.

"Haven't we seen enough eggs for one day?" Mom griped.

"It's a very strange egg," I insisted. "I can't identify it. I think — "

"Good night, Dana," Dad interrupted.

"Please don't ever mention eggs again," Mom added. "Promise?"

"Well, I . . ." I stared down at the pulsing green egg in my hand. "It'll only take a second. If you'll just — "

"Dana!" Dad yelled. "Why don't you go sit on it and hatch it?"

"Clark — don't talk to Dana that way!" Mom scolded.

"He's twelve years old. He can take a joke," Dad protested.

They started arguing about how Dad should talk to me.

I muttered good night and started back to my room.

I mean, I can take a hint.

Thump. Thump. The egg pulsed in my hand.

I had a sudden impulse to crack it open and see what was inside. But of course I would never do that.

I stopped outside Brandy's room. I was desperate to show my weird treasure to somebody. I knocked on her door.

No answer.

I knocked again, a little harder. Brandy is a very heavy sleeper.

Still no answer.

I started to knock a third time — and the door flew open. Brandy greeted me with an open-mouthed yawn. "What's wrong? Why'd you wake me?"

"I want to show you this egg," I told her.

She narrowed her eyes at me. "You're serious? After what happened at my party? After the worst birthday party in the history of America, you really want to show me an egg?"

I held it up. "Yeah. Here it is."

She slammed the door in my face.

"You mean you don't want to see it?" I called in.

No reply.

Once again, I could take a hint. I carried the egg back to my room and set it down carefully in the dresser drawer. Then I closed the drawer and climbed back into bed.

Thump. Thump. Thump.

I fell asleep to the steady throbbing.

The next morning, I woke up just in time to watch the egg hatch.

7

A loud cracking sound woke me up.

Blinking, I pulled myself up on one elbow. Still half-asleep, I thought I heard Brandy cracking her knuckles.

That's one of Brandy's secret talents. She never does it when adults are around. But when we're alone, she can crack out entire symphonies on her knuckles.

Another loud crack snapped me alert.

The dresser. The noises were coming from my dresser.

I heard a long *rip*, like Velcro ripping open. Then more cracks. Like cracking bones.

And I knew it had to be the egg.

My heart started to pound. I leaped up. Grabbed my glasses and slapped them onto my face. My legs got tangled in the bedsheet, and I nearly went sprawling over the floor.

I hurtled across the room. The egg was hatching — and I had to be there in time to watch.

I grabbed the drawer handles and eagerly pulled the drawer open. I was so eager, I nearly pulled the drawer out of the dresser!

Catching my balance, I gripped the dresser top with both hands and stared down at the egg.

Craaaaack.

The blue-and-purple veins throbbed. A long, jagged crack split across the green shell.

Unh unh.

I heard a low grunt from inside the egg. The grunt of a creature working hard to push out.

Unnnnnh.

What a struggle!

It doesn't sound like a turtle, I told myself. Is it some kind of exotic bird? Like a parrot? Or a flamingo maybe?

How would a flamingo egg get in my backyard?

How would *any* weird egg get in my backyard?

Unnnh unnnnh.

Craaaaack.

The sounds were really gross.

I rubbed my eyes and squinted down at the egg. It was bouncing and bobbing in the drawer now. Each grunt made the egg move.

The veins throbbed. Another crack split along the front of the shell. And thick yellow goo poured out into the drawer, seeping onto my socks.

"Yuck!" I cried.

The egg shook. Another crack. More of the thick liquid oozed down the egg and onto my socks.

The egg bobbed and bounced. I heard more hard grunting. *Unnnnh. Unnnnh.* The egg trembled with each grunt.

Yellow slime oozed as the cracks in the shell grew wider. The veins pulsed. The egg shook.

And then a large triangle of shell broke off. It fell into the drawer.

I leaned closer to stare into the hole in the egg. I couldn't really see what was inside. I could see only wet yellow blobby stuff.

Unnh unnnnh.

Another grunt — and the eggshell crackled and fell apart. Yellow liquid spilled into the drawer, soaking my socks.

I held my breath as a weird creature pushed itself out of the breaking shell. A yellow, lumpy thing.

A baby chicken?

No way.

I couldn't see a head. Or wings. Or feet.

I gripped the dresser top and stared down at it. The strange animal pushed away the last section of shell. This was amazing!

It rolled wetly over my socks.

A blob. A sticky, shiny yellow blob.

It looked like a pile of very runny scrambled eggs.

Except it had tiny green veins crisscrossing all over it.

My chest felt about to explode. I finally remembered to breathe. I let out my breath in a long whoosh. My heart was thudding.

The yellow blob throbbed. It made sick, wet sucking sounds.

It turned slowly. And I saw round black eyes near its top.

No head. No face. Just two tiny black eyes on top of the lumpy yellow body.

"You're not a chicken," I murmured out loud. My voice came out in a choked whisper. "You're definitely not a chicken."

But what was it?

"Hey — Mom! Dad!" I shouted.

They had to see this creature. They had to see the scientific discovery of the century!

"Mom! Dad! Hurry!"

No response.

The lumpy creature stared up at me. Throbbing. Its tiny green veins pulsing. Its eggy body bouncing.

"Mom? Dad?"

Silence.

I stared into my drawer.

What should I do?

8

I had to show it to Mom and Dad. I carefully closed the dresser drawer so it couldn't bounce out and escape. Then I went running downstairs, shouting at the top of my voice.

My pajama pants were twisted, and I nearly fell down the stairs. "Mom! Dad! Where *are* you?"

The house was silent. The vacuum cleaner had been pulled out of the closet. But no one was around to use it.

I burst into the kitchen. Were they still having breakfast?

"Mom? Dad? Brandy?"

No one there.

Sunlight streamed in through the kitchen window. The breakfast dishes — three cereal bowls and two coffee cups — were stacked beside the sink.

Where did they go? I wondered, my heart pounding. How could they leave when I had the

29

most amazing thing in the history of the known universe to show them?

I turned to leave the kitchen when I saw the note on the refrigerator. It was written in blue ink in Mom's handwriting. I snatched it off the magnet and read it:

"Dad and I took Brandy to her piano lesson. Make yourself some cereal. Love, M."

Cereal?

Cereal?

How could I think about cereal at a time like this?

What should I do now?

I leaned my forehead against the cool refrigerator, struggling to think. I couldn't leave the throbbing egg blob locked up in the dresser drawer all morning. Maybe it needed fresh air. Maybe it needed exercise. Maybe it needed food.

Food? I swallowed hard. What would it eat? What *could* it eat? It was just a lump of scrambled eggs with eyes.

I've got to take it out of there, I decided. I've got to show it to someone.

I thought instantly of Anne.

"Yes!" I exclaimed to myself. I'll take it next door and show it to Anne. She has a dog. She's really good with pets and animals. Maybe she'll have some idea of what I should do with it.

I hurried back upstairs and pulled on the jeans and T-shirt I had tossed on the floor the night before. Then I made my way to the dresser and slid open the drawer.

"Yuck!"

The egg blob sat in its own yellow slime. Its whole body throbbed. The tiny, round eyes stared up at me.

"I'm taking you to Anne's," I told it. "Maybe the two of us can figure out what you are."

Only one problem.

How do I take it there?

I rubbed my chin, staring down at it. Do I carry it on a plate? No. It might tumble off.

A bowl?

No. A jar?

No. It couldn't breathe.

A box.

Yes. I'll put it in a box, I decided. I opened my closet, dropped to my hands and knees, and shuffled through all the junk piled on the floor.

That's how I clean my room. I toss everything into the closet and shut the door. I have the cleanest room in the house. No problem.

The only problem is finding things in my closet. If I'm searching for something to wear, sometimes it takes a few days.

Today I got lucky. I found what I was looking for right away. It was a shoe box. The box my new sneakers came in.

I picked up the shoe box from the clutter and climbed to my feet. Then I kicked a bunch of stuff back into the closet so I could get the door closed.

"Okay!" I cried happily. I returned to the throbbing egg glob. "I'm carrying you to Anne's in this box. Ready?"

I didn't expect it to answer. And it didn't.

I pulled off the shoe box lid and set it on the dresser top. Then I lowered the box to the drawer.

"Now what?" I asked myself out loud.

How do I get it in the box? Do I just pick it up? Pick it up in my hand?

I held the box in my left hand and started to reach into the drawer with my right. But then I jerked my hand away.

Will it bite me? I wondered.

How can it? It doesn't have a mouth.

Will it sting me? Will it hurt me somehow?

My throat tightened. My hand started to tremble. It was so gross — so wet and eggy.

Pick it up, Dana, I told myself. Stop being such a wimp. You're a scientist — remember? You have to be bold. You have to be daring.

That's true, I knew. Scientists can't back away from something just because it's yucky and gross.

I took a deep breath.

I counted to three.

Then I reached for it.

9

As my hand moved toward it, the creature began to tremble. It shook like a glob of yellow Jell-O.

I pulled back once again.

I can't do it, I decided. I can't pick it up bare-handed. It might be too dangerous.

I watched it shake and throb. Wet bubbles formed on its eggy skin.

Is it scared of me? I wondered. Or is it trying to warn me away?

I had to find something to pick it up. I turned and glanced around the room. My eyes landed on my baseball glove tucked on the top shelf of my bookcase.

Maybe I could pick up the egg creature in the glove and drop it into the shoe box. I was halfway across the room when I decided I didn't want to get my glove all wet and gloppy.

I need to shovel it into the box, I thought.

A little shovel would make the job easy. I walked back to the dresser. The egg creature was still shaking like crazy. I closed the drawer. Maybe the darkness will calm it down, I thought.

I made my way down to the basement. Mom and Dad keep all their gardening supplies down there. I found a small metal trowel and carried it back up to my room.

When I pulled open the drawer, the eggy blob was still shaking. "Don't worry, fella," I told it. "I'm a scientist. I'll be real gentle."

I don't think it understood English. As I lowered the trowel into the drawer, the green veins on the throbbing body began to pulse.

The creature started bobbing up and down. The little black eyes bulged up at me. I had the feeling the little guy was about to explode or something.

"Easy. Easy," I whispered.

I lowered the trowel carefully beside it. Then I slowly, slowly slid it under the throbbing creature.

"There. Gotcha," I said softly.

It wiggled and shook on the blade of the trowel. I began to lift it carefully from the drawer.

The shoe box sat on the top of the dresser. I had the trowel in my right hand. I reached for the shoe box with my left.

Up, up. Slowly. Very slowly, I raised the egg creature toward the box.

Up. Up.

Almost to the box.

And the creature *growled* at me!

A low, gruff growl — like an angry dog.

"Ohhh!" I uttered a startled cry — and the trowel dropped from my hand.

"Yaaiii!" I let out another cry as it clanged across the floor — and the egg creature plopped wetly onto my sneaker.

"No!"

Without thinking, I bent down and grabbed it up in my hand.

I'm holding it! I realized, my heart pounding.

I'm holding it.

What's going to happen to me?

10

Nothing happened.

No shock jolted my body. No rash spread instantly over my skin. My hand didn't fall off.

The creature felt warm and soft, like runny scrambled eggs.

I realized I was squeezing it tightly. Too tightly? I loosened my grip.

And lowered it into the shoe box. And fastened the lid over the top.

I set the shoe box down on the dresser top and examined my hand. It felt wet and sticky. But the skin hadn't turned yellow or peeled off or anything.

I could hear the creature pulsing inside the box.

"Don't growl like that again," I told it. "You scared me."

I grabbed some tissues and wiped off my hand. I kept my eyes on the box. The creature was bouncing around in there.

What kind of animal is it? I wondered.

I wished Mom and Dad were home. I really, really wanted to show it to them.

I glanced at the clock radio on my bedside table. Only nine o'clock. Anne might still be sleeping. Sometimes she slept until noon on Saturdays. I'm not really sure why. She said it made the day go faster. Anne is a pretty weird girl.

I lifted the box with both hands. The egg creature felt surprisingly heavy. I made sure the lid was on tight. Then I carried it down the stairs and out the back door.

It was a sunny, warm day. A soft breeze made the fresh spring leaves tremble on the trees. Two houses down Mr. Simpson was already mowing his back lawn. Near the garage two robins were having a tug-of-war over a fat brown earthworm.

I carried the box to Anne's back door. The door was open. I peered through the screen.

"Hi, Dana. Come in," Anne's mother called from in front of the sink.

Balancing the box against my chest, I pulled open the screen door and stepped into the kitchen. Anne sat at the breakfast table. She wore a big blue T-shirt over black bike shorts. Her red-brown hair was tied behind her head in a long ponytail.

Three guesses what she was eating for breakfast.

You got it. Scrambled eggs.

"Yo, Dana!" she greeted me. "What's up?"

"Well — "

Mrs. Gravel moved to the stove. "Dana, have you had breakfast? Can I make you some scrambled eggs?"

My stomach did a flip-flop. I swallowed hard. "No. I don't think so."

"Nice fresh eggs," Mrs. Gravel insisted. "I could make them fried if you don't like scrambled."

"No thanks," I replied weakly.

I felt the eggy blob bounce inside the box.

"I might need some more," Anne told her mom, shoveling in a big glob. "These eggs are great, Mom."

Mrs. Gravel cracked an egg on the side of the skillet. "Maybe I'll make one for myself," she said.

All this egg talk was making me sick.

Anne finished her orange juice. "Hey — what's in the box? New sneakers?"

"Uh . . . no," I replied. "Check this out, Anne. You won't believe what I found."

I was so eager to show it to her! Holding the box in front of me with both hands, I started across the kitchen.

And tripped over Stubby.

Again!

That big dumb sheepdog always got underfoot.

"Whooooaaa!" I let out a cry as I fell over the dog — and watched the shoe box fly into the air.

I landed on top of Stubby. Got a mouthful of fur.

Struggled frantically to my feet.

And saw the egg creature sail out of the box and drop onto Anne's breakfast plate.

Anne's mouth dropped open. Her face twisted in disgust. "Oh, yuck!" she wailed. "Rotten eggs! Gross! Rotten eggs!"

"No — it's alive!" I protested.

But I don't think anyone heard me. Stubby jumped up on me as I started to explain, and nearly knocked me down again.

"Down, boy! Down!" Mrs. Gravel scolded. "You know better than that."

"Get this away!" Anne demanded, shoving her plate across the table.

Her mom examined the plate, then glared at me. "Dana, what's wrong with you? This isn't funny. You ruined perfectly good scrambled eggs."

"You spoiled my breakfast!" Anne cried angrily.

"No, wait — " I protested.

But I wasn't fast enough.

Mrs. Gravel grabbed up the plate. She carried it to the sink, clicked on the garbage disposal — and started to empty the egg creature into the roaring drain.

11

"Nooooo!"

I let out a shriek — and dove for the sink.

I made a wild grab and pulled the creature from the drain.

No. I pulled a handful of *scrambled eggs* from the drain!

The egg creature rolled around the sink and started to slide toward the gurgling drain. I tossed the scrambled eggs down and grabbed the creature as it started to drop toward the grinding blades.

The lumpy yellow blob felt hot in my hands. I could feel the veins throbbing. The whole creature pulsed rapidly, like a racing heart.

I raised it up to my face and examined it. Still in one piece. "I saved your life!" I told it. "Whew! What a close one!"

I balanced it carefully in my palm. It shuddered and throbbed. Wet bubbles rolled down its lumpy sides. The black eyes stared up at me.

"What *is* that thing?" Anne demanded, getting up from the breakfast table. She straightened her long ponytail. "Is it a puppet? Did you make it out of an old sock or something?"

Before I could answer, Mrs. Gravel gave me a gentle push toward the kitchen door. "Get it out of here, Dana," she ordered. "It's disgusting." She pointed down. "Look. It's dripping some kind of eggy goo all over my kitchen floor."

"I — I found it out back," I started. "I don't really know what it is, but — "

"Out," Anne's mom insisted. She held open the screen door for me. "Out. I mean it. I don't want to have to wash the whole floor."

I didn't have a choice. I carried the egg creature out into the backyard. It seemed a little calmer. At least it wasn't trembling and pulsing so hard.

Anne followed me to the driveway. The bright sun made the egg creature gleam. My hands felt slimy and wet. I didn't want to squeeze it too tightly. But I also didn't want to let it fall.

"Is it a puppet?" Anne demanded. She bent down to see it better. "Yuck. It's alive?"

I nodded. "I don't know what it is. But it's definitely alive. I found it yesterday. At Brandy's party."

Anne continued to study the yellow blob. "You found it? Where?"

"I found an egg back by the creek," I told her. "A very weird-looking egg. I took it home, and it hatched this morning. And this is what came out."

"But what *is* it?" Anne asked. She gingerly poked its side with a pointer finger. "Oh, yuck. It's wet and mushy."

"It's not a chicken," I replied.

"Duhhh," Anne said, rolling her eyes. "Did you figure that out all by yourself?"

"I thought it might be a turtle egg," I said, ignoring her sarcasm.

She squinted harder at it. "Do you think it's a turtle without its shell? Do turtles hatch without their shells?"

"I don't think so," I replied.

"Maybe it's some kind of mistake," Anne suggested. "A freak of nature. You know. Like you!" She laughed.

Anne has a great sense of humor.

She poked the egg creature again. The creature let out a soft wheeze of air. "Maybe you discovered a new species," Anne suggested. "A whole new kind of animal that's never been seen before."

"Maybe," I replied. That was an exciting idea.

"They'll name it after you," Anne teased. "They'll call it the Dodo!" She laughed again.

"You're not being very helpful," I said sharply.

And then I had an idea.

"Know what I'm going to do with it?" I said, cupping it carefully between my hands. "I'm going to take it to that little science lab."

She narrowed her eyes at me. "What science lab?"

"You know that little lab," I replied impatiently. "The one on Denver Street. Just three blocks from here."

"I don't hang out at weird little science labs," Anne said.

"Well, I don't, either," I told her. "But I've passed by that lab a million times, riding my bike to school. I'm going to take this thing there. Someone will tell me what it is."

"I'm not going with you," Anne said, crossing her skinny arms in front of her chest. "I have better things to do."

"I didn't invite you," I sneered.

She sneered back at me.

I think she was jealous that I found the mysterious creature and she didn't.

"Please get me the shoe box," I said. "I left it in your kitchen. I'm going to ride my bike over to that lab right now."

Anne went inside and came back with the shoe box. "It's all sticky inside," she said, making a disgusted face. "Whatever that thing is, it sure sweats a lot."

"Maybe your face scared it!" I declared. My turn to laugh. I'm usually the serious one. I don't get off too many jokes. But that was a pretty good one.

Anne ignored it. She watched as I lowered the creature into the box. Then she raised her eyes to me. "You sure that isn't some kind of wind-up toy? This thing is all a big joke — isn't it, Dana?"

I shook my head. "No way. It's no joke. I'll stop by later and tell you what the scientists at the lab say about it."

I fit the lid on the shoe box. Then I hurried to the garage to get my bike.

I couldn't wait to get to the science lab.

As it turned out, I should have stayed as far away from that place as possible.

But how could I know what was waiting for me there?

12

"Look out!"

Anne's stupid sheepdog ran in front of my bike just as I started down the driveway.

I jammed on the hand brake. My bike squealed to a sharp stop — and the shoe box nearly toppled off the handlebars.

"Stubby — you moron!" I shrieked.

The dog loped off across the backyard, probably laughing to himself. I think Stubby gets a real thrill by tripping me up whenever he sees me.

I waited for my heart to stop thudding in my chest. Then I steadied the shoe box on the handlebars.

I started pedaling along the street, steering with one hand, keeping the other hand on top of the box.

"The scientists at the lab have got to know what this thing is," I told myself. "They've *got* to."

I usually speed down my street. But this morning I pedaled slowly. I stopped at each corner to make sure no cars were coming.

I tried to steer away from bumps in the street. But my street has a lot of potholes. Each time I hit a bump, I could hear the egg creature bouncing inside the carton.

Just don't bounce out, I thought.

I pictured it bouncing out of the box, dropping onto the street, and being run over by a car.

I stopped to balance it better on the handlebars. Then I began pedaling slowly again.

Some kids from school were starting up a softball game on the playground on the next block. They called to me. I think they wanted me to join the game.

But I pretended I didn't hear them. I didn't have time for softball. I was on a scientific mission. I didn't look back. I kept pedaling.

As I turned the corner onto Denver, a city bus roared past. The whoosh of air from the bus nearly knocked me over.

As I steadied the bike, I saw the lid push up from the shoe box.

The egg creature was trying to escape!

I grabbed the box and tried to push down the lid. I pedaled faster. The lab was only a block away.

The creature pushed up against the lid.

I pushed back.

I didn't want to crush it. But I didn't want it to escape, either.

I could feel it bouncing inside the box. Pushing up against the lid.

I kept my hand on the lid, struggling to hold it down.

A station wagon filled with kids rumbled past. One of the kids yelled something to me. I didn't really hear him. I was concentrating as hard as I could on keeping the egg creature inside the box.

I rolled through a stop sign. I didn't even see it. Luckily no cars were approaching.

The lab came into view on the next corner. It was a white shingled building. Very low. Only one story tall. But very long. With a row of small, square windows along the front. It looked like a very long train car.

I bumped up the curb and rode my bike onto the grass. Then I grabbed the shoe box with both hands and hopped off. The bike fell to the ground, both wheels spinning.

Gripping the box tightly in both hands, I ran across the front lawn, up to the white double doors in front.

I found a doorbell on the wall to the right of the doors. I pushed it. Pushed it again. Kept my finger on it.

When no one came to the door, I tried the knob. Pushed. Then pulled.

No. The door was locked.

I tried knocking. I pounded as hard as I could with my fist.

Then I rang the bell again.

Where was everyone?

I was about to start pounding again when I saw the sign over the door. A small, hand-printed black-and-white sign that sent my heart sinking. It read:

CLOSED SATURDAYS AND SUNDAYS.

13

I let out a long sigh and shoved the box under my arm. I was so disappointed. What was I going to do with this weird egg creature now?

Shaking my head unhappily, I turned and started back to my bike. I was halfway across the grass when I heard the front door open.

I turned to see an older man in a white lab coat. He had shiny white hair, parted in the middle and slicked down on the sides. His moustache was salt-and-pepper. He had pale blue eyes that peered out at me from his pale, wrinkly face.

His smile made his eyes crinkle up at the sides. "Can I help you?" he asked.

"Uh . . . yeah," I stammered. I raised the shoe box in front of me and started back across the grass. I could feel the egg creature bouncing around in there.

"Is that a sick bird?" the man asked, squinting at the box. "I'm afraid I can't help you with that. This is a science lab. I'm not a vet."

"No. It's not a bird," I told him. I carried the box to the doorway. My heart was pounding. For some reason, I felt really nervous.

I guess I was excited about talking to a real scientist. I respect and admire scientists so much.

Also, I was excited about finally finding out what had hatched from that weird egg. And finding out what I should do with it.

The man smiled at me again. He had a warm, friendly smile that made me feel a little calmer. "Well, if it isn't a bird in there, what is it?" he asked softly.

"I was hoping you could tell me!" I replied. I shoved the shoe box toward him, but he didn't take it.

"It's something I found," I continued. "I mean, I found an egg. In my backyard."

"An egg? What kind of egg, son?"

"I don't know," I told him. "It was very big. And it had veins all over it. And it kind of breathed."

He stared at me. "An egg that breathed."

I nodded. "I put it in my dresser drawer. And then it hatched this morning. And — "

"Come in, son," the man said. "Come right in." His expression changed. His eyes flashed. He suddenly looked very interested.

He put a hand on my shoulder and guided me into the lab. I had to blink a few times and wait for my eyes to adjust to the dim light inside.

The walls were all white. I saw a desk and chairs. A low table with some science magazines on it. This was a waiting room, I decided. It was all very clean and modern-looking. A lot of chrome and glass and white leather.

The man had his eyes on the box in my hands. He rubbed his moustache with his fingers. "I'm Dr. Gray," he announced. "I'm the managing lab scientist here."

I switched the box to my left hand so I could shake hands with him. "I want to be a scientist when I'm older," I blurted out. I could feel my face turning red.

"What's your name, son?" Dr. Gray asked.

"Oh. Uh. Dana Johnson. I live a few blocks away. On Melrose."

"It's nice to meet you, Dana," Dr. Gray said, straightening the front of his white lab coat. He moved to the front door. He closed it, locked it, and bolted it.

That's weird, I thought, feeling a shiver of fear. Why did he do that?

Then I remembered that the lab was closed on weekends. He probably bolts the doors when the place is closed.

"Follow me," Dr. Gray said. He led the way down the narrow white hallway. I followed him into a small lab. I saw a long table cluttered with all kinds of test tubes, specimen jars, and electronic equipment.

51

"Set the box down there," he instructed, pointing to an empty spot on the table.

I set the box down. He reached in front of me to remove the lid. "You found this in your backyard?"

I nodded. "Back by the creek."

He carefully pulled the lid off the box.

"Oh my goodness!" he murmured.

14

The egg creature stared up at us. It quivered and bubbled against the side of the box. The bottom of the box was puddled with a sticky yellow goo.

"So you found one," Dr. Gray murmured, tilting the box. The yellow blob slid to the other end.

"Found one?" I replied. "You mean you know what it is?"

"I thought I rounded them all up," Dr. Gray replied, rubbing his moustache. He turned his pale blue eyes on me. "But I guess I missed one."

"What is it?" I demanded. "What kind of animal is it?"

He shrugged. He tilted the box the other way, making the egg creature slide to the other end. Then he gently poked the eggy blob in the back. "This is a young one," he said softly.

"A young *what*?" I asked impatiently.

"The eggs fell all over town," Dr. Gray said, poking the egg creature. "Like a meteor shower. Only on this town."

"Excuse me?" I cried. "They fell from the sky?" I wanted desperately to understand. But so far, nothing made sense.

Dr. Gray turned to me and put a hand on my shoulder. "We believe the eggs fell all the way from Mars, Dana. There was a big storm on Mars. Two years ago. It set off something like a meteor shower. The storm sent these eggs hurtling through space."

My mouth dropped open. I gazed down at the quivering yellow blob in the shoe box. "This — this is a *Martian*?" I stammered.

Dr. Gray smiled. "We think it came from Mars. We think the eggs flew through space for two years."

"But — but — " I sputtered. My heart was racing. My hands were suddenly ice cold.

Was I really staring at a creature from Mars?

Had I actually *touched* a Martian?

Then I had an even *weirder* thought: I found it. I picked it up from *my* backyard.

Did that mean it belonged to me?

Did I *own* a Martian?

Dr. Gray bounced the creature — *my* creature — in the box. Its veins pulsed. Its black eyes stared back at us. "We don't know how the eggs made it through the earth's atmosphere," the scientist continued.

"You mean they should have burned up?" I asked.

He nodded. "Most everything burns up when it hits our atmosphere. But the eggs seem to be very tough. So tough they weren't destroyed."

The egg creature made a gurgling sound. It plopped wetly against the side of the shoe box.

Dr. Gray chuckled. "This is a cute one."

"You have a lot of others?" I asked.

"Let me show you something, Dana." Holding the box in front of him, Dr. Gray led the way through a large metal door. The door clanged heavily behind us.

A long, narrow hallway — the walls painted white — led past several small rooms. Dr. Gray's lab coat made a starchy, scratchy sound as he walked. At the end of the hall, we stopped in front of a wide window.

"In there," Dr. Gray said softly.

I stared into the window.

Then I stared harder.

Was he crazy? Was he playing some kind of joke on me?

"I — I can't see anything at all!" I cried.

15

"Hold on a second. I forgot something," Dr. Gray said. He stepped over to the wall and flicked a light switch.

A light above our heads in the hallway flashed on. And now I could see through the window.

"Oh, wow!" I exclaimed as my eyes swept over the large room on the other side of the glass. I stared at a *crowd* of egg creatures!

Dozens of them.

Yellow, eggy blobs. All pulsing and quivering. Green veins throbbing.

The egg creatures huddled on the white tile floor. They looked like big globs of cookie dough on a baking sheet. Dozens of tiny, round black eyes stared out at us.

Unreal!

As I stared at them in amazement, I kept thinking they were like stuffed animals. But they weren't. They were alive. They breathed. They shook and bounced and bubbled.

"Would you like to go in?" Dr. Gray asked.

He didn't wait for me to answer. He pulled out a small black control unit from his pocket. He pushed a button, and the door swung open. Then he opened the door wider and guided me inside.

"Whoa!" I uttered a cry when I felt a blast of cold air. "It's *freezing* in here!" I exclaimed.

Dr. Gray smiled. "We keep it very cold. It seems to keep them more alert."

He held the shoe box in one hand. He motioned to the egg creatures with the other. "Once they hatch, the creatures don't like heat. If the temperature goes too high, they melt," he explained.

He lowered the box to the floor. "We don't want them to melt," he said. "If they melt, we can't study them."

Leaning over the box, he lifted my egg creature out gently. He placed it beside three or four other egg creatures. All of the yellow blobs began bouncing excitedly.

Dr. Gray picked up the box and stood back up. He smiled down at the new arrival. "We don't want you to melt, do we?" he told it. "We want you to be nice and alert. So we keep it as cold in here as we can."

I shivered and rubbed my arms. I had goosebumps all over my skin. From the excitement? Or from the cold?

I wished I had worn something warmer than a T-shirt!

The egg creatures bobbed and bubbled. I couldn't take my eyes off them. Real creatures from Mars!

I watched them start to bounce toward us. They moved surprisingly fast. They kind of rolled, kind of inched their way forward. They left slimy, yellow trails behind them as they moved.

I wanted to ask Dr. Gray a million questions. "Do they have brains?" I asked. "Are they smart? Can they communicate? Have you tried talking to them? Do they talk to each other? How can they breathe our air?"

He chuckled. "You have a good scientific mind, Dana," he said. "Let's take one question at a time. Which would you like me to answer first?"

"Well — " I started to reply. But I stopped when I realized what the egg creatures had done.

While Dr. Gray and I talked, they had all moved quickly into a circle.

And now they had the two of us surrounded.

I spun around.

The egg creatures had moved behind us. They blocked the door. And now they were closing in on us, bubbling and throbbing, leaving a trail of slime as they slid forward.

What were they planning to do?

16

In a panic, I turned to Dr. Gray. To my shock, he was grinning.

"They — they've trapped us!" I stammered.

He shook his head. "Sometimes they move like that. But don't be scared, Dana. They're harmless."

"Harmless?" I cried. My voice came out shrill and tiny. "But — but — "

"What can they do?" Dr. Gray asked, placing a comforting hand on my trembling shoulder. "They're only blobs of egg. They can't bite you — can they? They don't appear to have mouths. They can't grab you. Or punch you. Or kick you. They have no hands or legs."

The egg creatures moved their circle closer. I watched them, my throat still tight, my legs shaking.

I knew that what Dr. Gray was telling me was true.

But why were they doing this?

Why did they form a circle? Why were they closing in on us?

"Sometimes they form triangles," Dr. Gray told me. "Sometimes rectangles or squares. It's as if they're trying out different shapes they've seen. Maybe this is a way they're trying to communicate with us."

"Maybe," I agreed softly. I wished the egg creatures would back up. They were little, wet blobs. But they were really giving me the creeps!

I shivered again. My breath steamed up in front of me.

It was so cold, my glasses started to fog!

I stared down at the egg creature I had brought. It had joined the circle. It bobbed and bounced with all the others.

Dr. Gray turned and started to the door. I turned with him. I wanted to get out of that freezer as fast as I could!

"Thank you for bringing that one in," Dr. Gray said. He shook his head. "I thought I had collected them all. What a surprise that I missed one." He scratched his hair. "You say you found it in your backyard?"

I nodded. "It was an egg. But then it hatched in my dresser drawer." My teeth chattered. I was so cold!

"Does that mean it's mine?" I asked Dr. Gray. "I mean, does it belong to me?"

His smile faded. "I'm not really sure. I don't

know what the law is about alien creatures from outer space." He frowned. "Maybe there *is* no law."

I glanced down at the little blob. The green veins along its side were bulging. Its whole body was throbbing like crazy.

Was it sorry to see me go?

No way. That's really dumb, I told myself.

"I guess you'll want to keep it for a while and study it," I said to Dr. Gray.

He nodded. "Yes. I'm doing every kind of test I can think of."

"But can I come back and visit it?" I asked.

Dr. Gray narrowed his eyes at me. "Come back? Dana, what do you mean by come back? You're not leaving."

17

"Excuse me?" I choked out. I knew I hadn't heard him correctly.

My whole body shook in a wild shiver. I rubbed my bare arms, trying to warm them.

"Did you say I'm not leaving?" I managed to ask.

Dr. Gray locked his pale blue eyes on mine. "I'm afraid you can't leave, Dana. You must stay here."

A frightened cry escaped my throat. He wasn't serious! He couldn't be serious.

He can't keep me here, I told myself.

No way. He can't keep me here against my will. That's against the law.

"But . . . why?" I demanded weakly. "Why can't I go home?"

"You can understand — can't you?" Dr. Gray replied calmly. "We don't want anyone to know about these space aliens. We don't want anyone to know that we've been invaded by Martians."

He sighed. "You don't want to throw the whole world into a panic — do you, Dana?"

"I — I — I — " I tried to answer. But I was too frightened. Too startled. Too cold.

I glared angrily at Dr. Gray. "You have to let me go," I insisted in a trembling whisper.

His expression softened. "Please don't stare at me like that," he said. "I'm not a bad guy. I don't want to frighten you. And I don't want to keep you in this lab against your will. But what choice do I have? I'm a scientist, Dana. I have to do my job."

I stared back at him, my whole body shaking. I didn't know what to say. My eyes moved to the metal door. It was shut. But he hadn't bolted it.

I wondered if I could get to the door before he did.

"I have to study *you* too," Dr. Gray continued. He tucked his hands into the pockets of his lab coat. "It's my job, Dana."

"Study me?" I squeaked. "Why?"

He motioned to my egg creature. "You touched it — didn't you? You handled it? You picked it up?"

I shrugged. "Well, yeah. I picked it up. So what?"

"Well, we don't know what kind of dangerous germs it gave you," he replied. "We don't know what kind of germs or bacteria or strange diseases these things carried with them from Mars."

I swallowed hard. "Huh? Diseases?"

He scratched his moustache. "I don't want to scare you. You're probably perfectly okay. You feel okay — right?"

My teeth chattered. "Yeah. I guess. Just cold."

"Well, I have to keep you here and study you. You know. Watch you carefully. Make sure that touching the egg creature didn't harm you or change you."

No way, I thought.

I don't care about strange germs from Mars. I don't care about egg diseases. I don't care about science.

All I care about is getting out of here. Getting home to my family.

You're not keeping me here, Dr. Gray. You're not studying me.

Because I'm *outta* here!

Dr. Gray was saying something. I guess he was still explaining why he planned to keep me prisoner in this freezing cold lab.

But I didn't listen to him. Instead, I took off.

I ran toward the big metal door.

The circle of egg creatures blocked my way. But I leaped over them easily. And kept running.

Gasping for breath, shivering, I reached the door.

I grabbed the handle. And glanced back.

Was Dr. Gray chasing after me?

No. He hadn't moved.

Good! I thought. I caught him by surprise. I'm gone!

I turned the door handle. Pulled hard.

The door didn't open.

I pulled harder.

It didn't budge.

I tried pushing it.

No go.

Dr. Gray's voice rang in my ears. "The door is controlled electronically," he said calmly. "It's locked. It cannot be opened unless you have the control unit."

I didn't believe him. I tugged again. Then I pushed again.

He was telling the truth. The door was electronically sealed.

I gave up with a loud cry of protest. I spun around to face him. "How long do I have to stay here?" I demanded.

He replied in a low, icy voice. "Probably for a very long time."

18

"Step away from the door, Dana," Dr. Gray ordered. "Try to calm down."

Calm down?

"You'll be okay," the scientist said. "I take very good care of my specimens."

Specimens?

I didn't want to calm down. And I didn't want to be a specimen.

"I'm a boy. Not a specimen," I told him angrily.

I don't think he heard me. He lifted me out of the way. Then he clicked the small remote unit in his hand. The door opened just long enough for him to slide through.

It made a loud click as it snapped shut behind him.

Locked in. I was locked in this freezer with three dozen Martians.

My heart pounded. I heard a shrill whistle in my ears. My temples throbbed with pain. My whole head felt ready to explode!

I'd never been so angry in my life.

I let out a cry of rage.

The egg creatures all began to chatter. I spun around in surprise. They sounded a little like chimps.

A roomful of chimps, chattering away.

Only they weren't chimps. They were monsters from Mars. And I was locked in, all alone with them.

A specimen.

"Noooo!" I let out another howl and ran to the long window.

"You can't leave me here!" I shrieked. I pounded on the glass with both fists.

I wanted to cry. I wanted to scream until my throat was raw. I'd never felt so angry and so frightened all at once.

"Let me out! Dr. Gray — let me out of here! You can't keep me here!" I screamed. I banged on the window as hard as I could.

I'll pound till I break the glass, I told myself.

I'll break through. Then I'll climb out and escape.

I beat my fists frantically against the glass. "Let me *out* of here! You can't *do* this!"

The glass was thick and hard. No way I could break through.

"*Let me out!*" I uttered a final scream.

When I turned back into the room, the egg creatures stopped chattering. They stared up at me with their black, button eyes.

They didn't quiver or bounce. They stood totally still. As if they had frozen.

I'm going to freeze! I realized. I rubbed my bare arms. But it didn't help warm me. My hands were ice cold.

Icicles are going to form on me, I thought. I'm going to freeze to death in here. I'm going to turn into a human Popsicle.

The egg creatures stood so still. Their eyes were all locked on me. As if they were studying me. As if they were trying to decide what to do about me.

Suddenly my egg creature broke the silence. I recognized it by the blue veins down its front. It started to chatter loudly.

The other egg creatures turned, as if listening to it.

Was it talking to them? Was it communicating in some weird Martian chatter language?

"I hope you're telling them all how I saved your life!" I called to it. "I hope you're telling them what a good guy I am. You almost went down the drain — remember?"

Of course the egg creature couldn't understand me.

I don't know why I was shouting at it like that. I guess I was totally losing it. Totally freaked.

As the egg creature chattered on, I stared at

the others. They all listened in silence. I started to count them. There were so many of them — and so *few* of me!

Were they friendly? Did they like strangers? Did they like humans?

How did *they* feel about being locked up in this freezing cold room?

Did they feel anything at all?

These were questions I didn't really want to know the answers to.

I just wanted to get out of there.

I decided to try the window again. But before I could move, my egg creature stopped talking.

And the others started to move.

Silently, they huddled together. Pressed together into a wide yellow wedge.

And rolling faster than I could imagine, they attacked.

19

"Hey — !" I uttered a startled cry and backed up.

The wedge of egg creatures rolled forward. Their bodies slapped the floor wetly as they bounced toward me.

I retreated until my back hit the window.

Nowhere to run.

"What do you want?" I screamed. My voice came out high and tight in panic. "What are you going to do?"

I turned and banged on the window again, pounding with open hands. "Dr. Gray! Dr. Gray! Help me!"

Did they plan to roll over me? To swallow me up?

To my surprise, the egg creatures stopped a few inches in front of me. They twirled and bounced until they had formed a circle once again.

Then, moving quickly and silently, they shifted back into a big yellow triangle.

I stared down at them, shivering, my teeth chattering.

They're not attacking, I decided.

But what *are* they doing?

Why are they forming these shapes? Are they trying to *talk* to me?

I took a deep breath, trying to calm my panic.

You're a scientist, Dana, I reminded myself. Act like a scientist. Not a frightened kid. Try to talk back to them.

I thought hard for a few seconds. Then I raised my hands in front of me. And I formed a circle with my pointer fingers and thumbs.

I held the circle up so the egg creatures could all see it. And waited to see if they did anything.

The yellow blobs had formed a wide triangle that nearly filled the room. I saw their round black eyes go up to the circle I had formed.

And then I watched them bounce and roll — into a circle!

Were they copying me?

I straightened my fingers and thumbs into a triangle.

And the egg creatures formed a triangle.

Yes!

We're communicating! I realized. We're talking to each other!

I suddenly felt really excited. I felt like some kind of pioneer.

I'm the first person on earth to communicate with Martians! I told myself.

These creatures are friendly, I decided. They're not dangerous.

I didn't really know that for sure. But I was so excited that I had communicated with them, I didn't want to think anything bad about them.

Dr. Gray has no right to keep them prisoner here, I thought.

And he has no right to lock me up with them.

I didn't believe his excuse for keeping me here. Not for a minute.

Just because I touched one? Just because I handled one?

Did he really expect me to believe that touching an egg creature could harm me?

Did he really think it would rot my skin off or something?

Did he really think that touching an egg creature would give me a weird disease or change me in some way?

That was just stupid.

I carried that little yellow blob in my hands — and I felt perfectly fine.

These creatures are my friends, I told myself. Touching them isn't going to harm me in any way.

But I'm a scientist. At least, I want to be a scientist. So I have to be scientific, I realized.

I decided to check myself out — just to make sure.

I raised my hands and inspected them carefully, first one, then the other. They looked okay to me. No strange rashes. No skin peeling off. I still had four fingers and a thumb on each hand.

I rubbed my arms. They were the same too. Perfectly okay.

Might as well check myself out all over, I told myself.

I reached down and grabbed my left leg.

Soft and mushy!

"Oh no!" I wailed.

I squeezed my leg again. Soft and lumpy.

I didn't have to look. I knew what was happening.

I was slowly turning into one of them. I was turning into a lump of scrambled eggs!

20

"No. Oh, please — no."

I squeezed my mushy ankle. I couldn't bear to look down. I didn't want to see what was happening to me.

But I had to.

Slowly, I lowered my gaze.

And saw that I was squeezing one of the egg creatures. Not my leg.

I let go instantly and raised my hand. A relieved laugh escaped my throat.

"Oh wow!"

How could I think that mushy blob was my leg?

I watched the little Martian scurry back to its pals.

I shook my head. Even though no one else was around, I felt like a total jerk.

Just calm down, Dana, I scolded myself.

But how could I?

The air in the lab seemed to get colder. I couldn't

stop shivering. I clamped my jaws tightly. But I couldn't stop my teeth from chattering.

I squeezed my nose. Cold and numb. I rubbed my ears. They were numb too.

This is no joke, I thought, my throat tightening. I'm going to get frostbite. I'm really going to freeze.

I tried thinking warm thoughts. I thought about the beach in summer. I thought about a blazing fire in the fireplace in our den.

It didn't help.

A hard shiver made my whole body twitch.

I've got to do something to take my mind off the cold, I decided.

The egg creatures had spread out over the room. I raised my hands again and formed a triangle.

They stared up at it, but didn't move.

I curled my fingers into a circle.

They ignored this one too.

"I guess you guys got bored, huh?" I asked them.

I tried to bend my fingers and thumbs into a rectangle. But it was too hard. Fingers and thumbs can't really bend into a rectangle.

Besides, the egg creatures weren't paying much attention to me.

I'm going to freeze, I told myself again. Freeze. Freeze. Freeze. The word repeated in my mind until it became an unhappy chant.

I lowered myself to the floor and pressed into the corner. I curled up, trying to save body warmth. Or what was left of it.

A sound on the other side of the window made me jump up.

Someone was coming. Dr. Gray? To let me out?

I turned eagerly to the door. I heard footsteps out in the hall. Then a clink of metal.

A slot opened just above the floor to the left of the door. A food tray slid in. It plopped onto the floor.

I hurried over to it. Macaroni and cheese and a small container of milk.

"But I *hate* macaroni and cheese!" I screeched.

No reply.

"I hate it! I hate it! I hate it!" I wailed.

I was starting to lose it again. But I didn't care.

I leaned over the tray and held my hands over the plate of macaroni. The steam warmed my hands.

At least it's hot, I thought.

I sat down on the floor and lifted the tray to my lap. Then I gulped down the macaroni, just for the warmth.

It tasted horrible. I hate that wet, clotted, cheesy taste. But it did warm me up a little.

I didn't open the milk. Too cold.

Feeling a little better, I shoved the tray aside and climbed to my feet. I strode over to the window and started pounding the glass with my fists.

"Dr. Gray — let me out!" I shouted. "Dr. Gray — I know you can hear me. Let me out! You can't lock me in here and make me eat macaroni and cheese! Let me out!"

I screamed until my voice was hoarse. I didn't hear a reply. Not a sound from the other side of the glass.

I turned away from the window in disgust.

"I've got to find a way out of here," I said out loud. "I've *got* to!"

And then, I had an idea.

21

Sad to say, it was a bad idea.

The kind of idea you think of when you're freezing to death in a total panic.

What was the idea? To call home and tell Mom and Dad to come get me.

The only problem with that idea was that there were no phones in the room.

I searched carefully. There were metal shelves up to the ceiling against the back wall. They contained only scientific books and files. There was a desk in one corner. The desktop was bare.

Nothing else.

Nothing else in the whole room. Except for the dozens of egg creatures and me.

I needed another idea, an idea that didn't call for a telephone.

But I was stumped. I tried the door again. I thought Dr. Gray might have gotten careless and left it unlocked.

No such luck.

I checked out the slot where my food tray had been delivered. It was only a few inches tall. Way too narrow for me to slip through.

I was trapped. A prisoner. A specimen.

I dropped glumly down to the floor and rested my back against the wall. I pulled up my knees and wrapped my arms around them. I curled into a ball, trying to stay warm.

How long did Dr. Gray plan to keep me here? Forever?

I let out a miserable sigh. But then a thought helped to cheer me. I suddenly had a little hope.

I remembered something I had forgotten. I had told Anne where I was going!

This morning in her backyard, I had told Anne I was going to take the egg creature to the science lab.

I'm going to be rescued! I realized.

I leaped to my feet and shot both fists into the air. I opened my mouth in a happy cheer. "Yesssss!"

I knew exactly what would happen.

When I don't show up for dinner, Mom or Dad will call Anne. Because that's where I'm always hanging out when I should be home for dinner.

Anne will tell them I went to the science lab on Denver.

Mom will say, "He should be back by now."

Dad will say, "I'd better go get him."

And Dad will come and rescue me.

Only a matter of time, I knew. Only a matter of a few hours, and Dad will be here to get me out of this freezer.

I felt so much better.

I lowered myself back to the floor and leaned against the wall to wait. The egg creatures all stared at me. Watched me in silence. Trying to figure me out, I guess.

I didn't realize that I fell asleep. I guess I was worn out from all the excitement — and the fear.

I'm not sure how long I slept.

Voices woke me up. Voices from out in the hall.

I sat up, instantly alert. And I listened.

And heard Dad's voice.

Yes!

He was here. He was about to rescue me.

Yes!

I climbed to my feet. I stretched. I got ready to greet Dad.

And then, from the front hall, I heard Dr. Gray say, "I'm sorry, Mr. Johnson. Your son never stopped here."

22

"Are you sure?" I heard Dad ask.

"Very sure," Dr. Gray replied. "I'm the only one here today. We're closed. We had no visitors."

"He's about this tall," I heard Dad say. "He has dark hair, and he wears glasses."

"No. Sorry," Dr. Gray insisted.

"But he told his friend that he was coming here. He had something he wanted to show to a scientist. His bike is gone from the garage."

"Well, you can check outside for your son's bike," Dr. Gray told Dad. "But I don't think you'll find it."

He moved it! I realized. Dr. Gray moved my bike so no one would find it!

I let out a shout of rage and ran to the window. "Dad — I'm in here!" I shouted. I cupped my hands around my mouth so my voice would be even louder. "Dad! Can you hear me? I'm in here! Dad?"

I took a deep breath and listened. My heart was

thudding so loudly, I could barely hear their voices from the front.

Dad and Dr. Gray continued talking in low, calm voices.

"Dad! Can't you hear me?" I screamed. "It's me, Dana! Come back here, Dad! I'm here! Come let me out!"

My voice cracked. My throat ached from screaming so loud.

"Dad — *please!*"

My chest heaving, I pressed my ear against the window and listened again.

"Well, it's very strange, Mr. Johnson," Dr. Gray was saying. "The boy never came here. Would you like to look around the lab?"

Yes, Dad! I pleaded silently. *Say yes.*

Tell him that you'd like to look around the lab, Dad! Please!

"No, thanks," I heard Dad say. "I'd better keep searching. Thank you, Dr. Gray."

I heard Dad say good-bye.

I heard the front door close.

And I knew I was doomed.

23

"I don't believe this," I murmured out loud. "Dad was so close. So close!"

I sank back to the floor. I felt as if my heart were sinking too. I wanted to keep dropping, down onto the floor, into the ground. Just keep sinking till I disappeared forever.

My throat ached from screaming. Why couldn't Dad hear me? I could hear him.

And why did he believe Dr. Gray's lies? Why didn't Dad check out the lab for himself?

He would see me through the window. And I would be rescued.

Dr. Gray is evil, I realized. He pretends to be interested only in science. He pretended to be worried about my health, about my safety. He said that's why he was keeping me here — to make sure I was safe.

But he lied to my father.

And he was lying to me.

Crouched on the floor, I shivered as the frigid air seemed to seep right through my skin. I shut my eyes and lowered my head.

I wanted to stay calm. I knew I had to stay calm to think clearly. But I couldn't. The chills I felt running down my back weren't just from the cold. They were also from terror.

Voices in the front snapped me to attention. I held my breath and listened.

Was that my dad?

Or was I starting to hear things?

"Maybe I *will* take a look around." That's what I thought I heard Dad say.

Was I dreaming it?

No. I heard Dr. Gray mumble something. Then I heard Dad say, "Sometimes Dana sneaks into places where he doesn't belong. He's so interested in science, he may have sneaked in through a back door, Dr. Gray."

"Yes!" I cried happily. Every time I lost all hope, I somehow got another chance.

I jumped up and hurried to the window. I crossed my fingers and prayed Dad would walk to the back and see me.

After a few seconds, I saw Dad and Dr. Gray at the far end of the long, white hall. Dr. Gray was leading him slowly, opening doors. They peered into each lab, then moved on.

"Dad!" I called. "Can you hear me? I'm back here!"

Even though I had my face pressed up to the window glass, he couldn't hear me.

I banged on the glass. Dad kept walking with Dr. Gray. He didn't look up.

I waited for them to come closer. My heart was banging against my chest now. My mouth was dry. I pressed up close to the window.

In a few seconds, Dad would peer into the window and see me standing here.

And then I would be out — and Dr. Gray would have some real explaining to do.

With my hands and nose pressed against the glass, I watched them move forward. The hall was dark on this end. But I could see them clearly as they peeked into the labs at the other end.

"Dad!" I shouted. "Dad — over here!"

I knew he couldn't hear me. But I had to shout anyway.

The two men disappeared into a lab for a few seconds. Then they came out and stepped toward me.

They were talking in low tones. I couldn't hear what they were saying.

Dad had his eyes on Dr. Gray.

Turn this way, Dad, I silently urged. *Please — look to the end of the hall. Look in the window.*

Chatting softly, they disappeared through another door.

What on earth are they talking about? I wondered.

A few seconds later, they were back in the hall. Moving this way.

Dad — please! Here I am! I pressed up eagerly against the glass.

I pounded my fists on the window.

Dad looked up.

And stared into the window.

He stared right at me.

I'm rescued! I realized.

I'm *outta* here!

Dad stared at me for a few seconds.

Then he turned back to Dr. Gray. "Thanks for showing me around," he said. "Dana definitely isn't here. Sorry I wasted your time."

24

"Dad — I'm right here!" I shrieked. "You're look-ing right at me!"

Was I invisible?

Why didn't he see me?

"Sorry I wasted your time, Dr. Gray," I heard Dad say again.

"Good luck in finding Dana," Dr. Gray replied. "I'm sure he'll turn up really soon. He's probably at a friend's house and forgot the time. You know how kids are."

"Nooooooo!" I let out a long wail. "Dad — come back! Dad!"

As I stared in horror, Dad turned away and started back down the long hall.

With another cry, I began to pound on the win-dow glass with both fists. "Dad! Dad! Dad!" I chanted with each slam of my fist.

Dad turned around. "What's that noise?" he asked Dr. Gray.

Dr. Gray turned too.

I pounded the glass even harder. I pounded until my knuckles were raw and throbbing. "Dad! Dad! Dad!" I continued to chant.

"What's that pounding noise?" Dad demanded from halfway down the hall.

"It's the pipes," Dr. Gray told him. "I've been having a lot of trouble with the pipes. The plumber is coming on Monday."

Dad nodded.

He kept walking. I heard him say good-bye to the scientist. Then I heard the door close behind him.

I knew that this time he wouldn't come back.

I didn't move from the window. I stared through the glass down the long hall.

A few seconds later, I saw Dr. Gray coming toward me. He had an angry scowl on his face.

I'm his prisoner now, I thought glumly.

What does he plan to do?

25

He stopped outside the window. He clicked on the hall light.

In the bright light, I could see beads of sweat on his forehead. He frowned and stared in at me with those cold blue eyes.

"Nice try, Dana," he said sourly.

"Huh? What do you mean?" I choked out. My legs were trembling. Not from the cold. I was really terrified now.

"You almost got your father's attention," Dr. Gray replied. "That wouldn't have been nice. That would have spoiled my plans."

I pressed both palms against the glass. I tried to force myself to stop trembling.

"Why couldn't Dad see me?" I demanded.

Dr. Gray rubbed a hand over his side of the window. "It's one-way glass," he explained. "No one can see into the room from the hall — unless I turn on the bright hall light."

I let out a long sigh. "You mean — ?"

"Your father saw only blackness," the scientist said with a pleased grin. "He thought he was staring into an empty room. Just the way you did — until I turned on the light."

"But why didn't he hear me?" I demanded. "I was shouting my head off."

Dr. Gray shook his head. "A waste of time. The room you are in is totally soundproof. Not a sound escapes into the hall."

"But I can hear you!" I declared. "I could hear every word you and Dad said. And now you can hear me."

"There is a speaker system in the wall," he explained. "I can turn it on and off with the same control unit that locks the door."

"So I could hear you, but you couldn't hear me," I murmured.

"You're a very smart boy," he replied. His blue eyes flashed. "I know you're smart enough not to try any more tricks in there."

"You have to let me out!" I screamed. "You can't keep me here!"

"Yes, I can," he replied softly. "I can keep you here as long as I like, Dana."

"But — but — " I sputtered. I was so frightened, I couldn't speak.

"It's my duty to keep you in there," Dr. Gray said calmly. He didn't care that I was so scared and upset. He didn't care about me at all, I realized.

He must be crazy, I decided.

Crazy and evil.

"It's my duty to keep you here," he repeated. "I must make sure that the egg creatures haven't harmed you. I must make sure that the egg creatures haven't given you strange germs that you might pass on to others."

"Let me out!" I shrieked. I was too frightened and angry to argue with him now. Too angry and frightened to think clearly. "Let me out! Let me out!" I demanded, pounding on the glass with my aching fists.

"Get some rest, Dana," he instructed. "Don't tire yourself out, son. I want to start doing tests on you in the morning. I have many, many tests to perform."

"But I'm f-freezing!" I stammered. "Let me out of here. At least let me stay somewhere warm. Please?"

He ignored my plea. He clicked off the hall light and turned away.

I watched him make his way down the long hall. He disappeared through a door in front. And closed the door hard behind him.

I stood there, trembling, my heart pounding.

I was cold — and very scared.

I had no way of knowing things were about to get a *lot* scarier!

26

I was so desperate to get Dad's attention, I nearly forgot about the egg creatures. Now I turned from the window to find them scattered around the room.

They stood still as statues. They didn't bounce or quiver. They all seemed to be staring at me.

Dr. Gray had turned off all the lights except for a tiny, dim bulb in the ceiling. The little egg blobs appeared pale and gray in the dim light.

I felt a chill at the back of my neck.

Was it safe to go to sleep in the same room with them?

I suddenly felt exhausted. So tired that all my muscles ached. My head spun.

I needed sleep.

I knew I had to rest so I could be alert and sharp tomorrow. Alert and sharp so I could find a way to escape.

But if I fell asleep, what would the egg creatures do?

Would they leave me alone? Would they sleep too?

Or would they try to harm me in some way?

Were they good? Were they evil?

Were they intelligent at all?

I had no way of knowing.

I only knew I couldn't stay awake much longer.

I dropped down to the floor and curled up in the corner. I tried to stay warm by tucking myself into a ball.

But it didn't help. The cold swept over me. My nose was frozen. My ears were numb. My glasses were frozen to my face.

Even wrapped up tightly, I couldn't stop shaking.

I'm going to freeze to death, I realized.

When Dr. Gray comes back tomorrow morning, he'll find me on the floor. A solid lump of ice.

I gazed at the egg creatures. They stared back at me in the dim light.

Silence.

Such heavy silence in the room that I wanted to scream.

"Aren't you cold?" I cried out to them. My voice came out hoarse, weak from all the screaming I had done. "Aren't you freezing to death too?" I asked them. "How can you guys stand it?"

Of course they didn't reply.

"Dana, you're totally losing it," I scolded myself out loud.

I was trying to talk to a bunch of egg lumps from another planet! Did I really expect them to answer me?

They stared back in silence. None of them quivered. None of them moved. Their little dark eyes glowed in the dim light from the ceiling.

Maybe they're asleep, I thought.

Maybe they sleep with their eyes open. That's why they're not moving. That's why they've stopped bouncing. They're sound asleep.

That made me feel a little better.

I tucked myself into a tighter ball, and I tried to fall asleep too. If only I could stop shivering.

I closed my eyes and silently repeated the word, "sleep, sleep, sleep" in my mind.

It didn't help.

And when I opened my eyes, I saw the egg creatures start to move.

I was wrong. They weren't asleep.

They were wide awake. And they were all moving together. All moving at once.

Coming to get me.

27

"Ohhh." A low moan escaped from my throat.

I was already shaking all over from the cold. But now my entire body shuddered from fear.

The egg creatures moved with surprising speed.

They were bunching together in the center of the room. Pressing into each other, making wet smacking sounds.

I tried to climb to my feet. But my legs didn't work.

My knees bent like rubber, and I landed back on the floor. I pressed back into the corner — and watched them move.

They slapped up against each other. Loud, wet slaps.

And as they pushed together, they rolled forward. Rolled toward me.

"What are you doing?" I cried in a high, shrill voice. "What are you going to do to me?"

They didn't reply.

The wet smacks echoed through the room as the eggy creatures threw themselves into each other.

"Leave me alone!" I shrieked. Once again I tried to stand. I made it to my knees. But I was trembling too hard to balance on two feet.

"Leave me alone — please! I'll help you guys escape too!" I promised. "Really. I'll help you escape — tomorrow. Just let me make it through the night."

They didn't seem to understand.

They didn't seem to hear me!

What are they doing? I asked myself, watching them creep forward. Why are they doing this?

They had waited until I nearly fell asleep, I realized.

That means they wanted to catch me off guard. They wanted to sneak up on me.

Because they were about to do something I wasn't going to like. Something I wasn't going to like at all.

I pressed my back against the wall.

The egg creatures moved quickly now, pale in the gray light.

Squinting hard at them, I realized to my horror that they had all stuck themselves together.

They were no longer dozens of little egg creatures.

Now they had joined together to form *one enormous egg creature!*

I was staring at a big, quivering *wall* of egg! A wall so big it nearly covered the floor of the room.

A wall that was rolling toward me. Rolling to get me.

"Whoa! Please — whoa!" I choked out.

I knew I should climb to my feet. I knew I should try to run.

But where could I run?

How could I escape from this huge, solid egg wall?

I couldn't.

So I lay there and watched it come. Too frozen. Too frozen to move.

"Ohhhh." I moaned as the front of the wall of eggs rose up over my shoes.

It was moving so fast now. Crawling somehow. Crawling over me.

The egg wall swept over my shoes. Over the legs of my jeans. Over my waist.

I lay there helpless as it swept over me.

Too frozen. Too frozen.

Helpless, as it poured over me.

Trapping me beneath it.

Smothering me.

28

I should have moved.

I should have fought it.

Too late. Too late now.

The sticky, warm egg creatures — all glued together — rolled over me like a heavy carpet.

I pushed up both arms. I raised my knees. I tried to squirm away.

Too late.

I tried to roll out from underneath. But the heavy, living carpet had me pinned on my back. Pinned to the floor.

It rolled over my waist. And then quickly, over my chest.

Was it going to sweep over my head? Was it going to smother me?

I punched at it with both fists.

But it was too late to push it away. Too late to do it any harm.

Too late to stop it as it crept closer to my neck. So warm and heavy.

I twisted my head from side to side. I tried to roll away.

But it was no use.

Too late. Too late to fight back.

And now I lay there, trapped. And felt it creep up to my chin.

Felt it throbbing. Pulsing.

Dozens of eggy monsters all pressed together. Alive. A living sheet of egg creatures. Covering me.

Covering me.

I took a deep breath and held it as the heavy, warm carpet pressed itself against my chin. My arms and legs were pinned to the floor. I couldn't squirm away.

I couldn't move.

To my surprise, the egg carpet stopped under my chin.

I let out a long whoosh of air.

And waited.

Had it really stopped?

Yes.

It didn't crawl over my head. It rested heavily on top of me. Throbbing steadily, as if it had two dozen heartbeats.

So warm.

I felt so warm beneath it. Almost cozy.

I let out a sigh. For the first time, I had stopped shivering. My hands and feet were no longer frozen. No chills ran down my back.

Warm. I felt toasty and warm.

A smile spread over my face. I could feel my fear fading away with the cold.

The egg creatures weren't trying to harm me, I realized.

They wanted to help me.

They pressed themselves together to form a blanket. A warm and cozy blanket.

They worked together to keep me from freezing.

They saved my life!

With the warm, pulsing blanket on top of me, I suddenly felt calm. And sleepy. I drifted into a peaceful, dreamless sleep.

Such a wonderful, soothing sleep.

But it didn't help get me ready for the horrors of the next morning.

29

I awoke a couple of times during the night. At first, I felt alarmed and frightened when I saw that I wasn't home in bed.

But the pulsing, warm egg blanket relaxed me. I shut my eyes and drifted back to sleep.

Some time in the morning, I was aroused from a deep sleep by an angry voice. I felt hands grab my shoulders roughly.

Someone was shaking me hard. Shaking me awake.

I opened my eyes to find Dr. Gray bending over me in his white lab coat. His face was twisted in anger. He shook me hard, shouting furiously.

"Dana — what have you done? What have you done to the egg monsters?"

"Huh?" I was still half asleep. My eyes struggled to focus. My head bobbed loosely on my shoulders as the angry scientist shook me.

"Let go!" I finally managed to choke out.

"What have you done to them?" Dr. Gray de-

101

manded. "How did you turn them into a blanket?"

"I — I didn't!" I stammered.

He uttered a furious growl. "You've ruined everything!" he shrieked.

"Please — " I started, struggling to wake up.

He let go of me and grabbed the egg blanket in both hands. "What have you done, Dana?" he repeated. "Why did you do this?"

With another cry of rage, he ripped the blanket off me — and heaved it against the wall.

The egg creatures made a soft *splat* as they hit the lab wall. I heard them utter tiny squeals of pain. The blanket folded limply to the floor.

"You shouldn't do that, Dr. Gray!" I screamed, finally finding my voice. I jumped to my feet. I could still feel the warmth of the egg blanket on my skin.

"You hurt them!" I shrieked.

I gazed down at the yellow blanket. It bubbled silently where it had been thrown. It didn't move.

"You let them touch you?" Dr. Gray demanded, twisting his face in disgust. "You let them cover you up?"

"They saved my life!" I declared. "They pushed together to make a warm blanket — and they saved my life!"

I glanced down again. The egg creatures remained stuck together. The blanket appeared to be seething now. Throbbing hard. As if excited. Or angry.

"Are you crazy?" Dr. Gray cried, his face red with anger. "Are you crazy? You let these *monsters* rest on top of you? You touched them? You handled them? Are you trying to destroy my discovery? Are you trying to destroy my work?"

He's the crazy one, I realized. Dr. Gray isn't making any sense. He isn't making any sense at all.

He moved quickly — and grabbed me again. Held me in a tight grip so I couldn't escape. And pulled me to the door.

"Let go of me! Where are you taking me?" I demanded.

"I thought you could be trusted," Dr. Gray replied in a menacing growl. "But I was wrong. I'm so sorry, Dana. So sorry. I had hoped to keep you alive. But I see now that is impossible."

30

He dragged me to the door. He stopped and reached into the pocket of his lab coat. Reached for the control unit to open the door.

I saw my chance. He had me by only one hand. With a hard burst of strength, I pulled away. He let out a cry. Reached both hands for me. Missed.

I ran to the other side of the lab. I turned at the wall to face him.

He had a strange smile on his face. "Dana, there's nowhere to run," he said softly.

My eyes flashed around the room. I don't know what I was searching for. I had seen it all. And I knew that he was telling the truth.

Dr. Gray stood blocking the only door. The long window was too heavy and thick to break through. And it didn't open.

There were no other windows. No other doors. No ways to escape.

"What are you going to do now, Dana?" Dr. Gray asked softly, the strange smile stuck on his face. His blue eyes locked coldly on mine. "Where are you going to go?"

I opened my mouth to reply. But I had nothing to say.

"I'll tell you what's going to happen," Dr. Gray said softly, calmly. "You're going to stay in here. In this cold, cold room. I'm going to leave you now and make sure you're locked in."

His smile grew wider. "Then do you know what I'm going to do? Do you?"

"What?" I choked out.

"I'm going to make it colder in here. I'm going to make it colder than a freezer."

"No — !" I protested.

His smile faded. "I trusted you, Dana. I trusted you. But you broke that trust. You let them touch you. You let them form this — this carpet! You ruined them, Dana! You ruined my egg monsters!"

"I — I didn't do anything!" I stammered. I balled my hands into fists. But I felt so helpless. Helpless and afraid.

"You can't freeze me in here!" I cried. "I didn't do anything! You can't leave me in here to freeze!"

"Of course I can," Dr. Gray replied coldly. "This is my lab. My own little world. I can do whatever I want."

He pulled the little black remote unit from his lab coat pocket. He pointed it at the door and pushed a button.

The door swung open.

He started to leave. "Good-bye, Dana," he called.

31

"No — stop!" I called.

Dr. Gray turned from the doorway.

And as he turned, the blanket of egg creatures rose up.

It stood straight up — and flung itself over him. It dropped on top of the scientist with a hard *thud*.

"Hey — " He let out an angry cry. The cry was muffled by the heavy yellow blanket of egg creatures.

The egg blanket covered him. I watched him struggle underneath it. And I listened to his muffled cries.

He was squirming and twisting beneath the blanket. But he couldn't toss it off. And he couldn't slide out from under it.

He crumpled to the floor, and the blanket crumpled with him.

I watched it seething and bubbling on top of him.

Then I didn't wait another second. I took a deep breath — and I ran across the room. I darted past the egg blanket with Dr. Gray twisting and thrashing underneath it.

Out the door.

Down the long hall to the front of the lab.

Yes! A few seconds later, I pushed open the front door and burst outside. Breathing hard, sucking in the sweet, fresh air.

A beautiful morning. A red ball of a sun still rising over the spring-green trees. The sky clear and blue.

I glanced around. I could see a paperboy on his bike halfway up the block. No one else on the street.

I turned and ran around to the side of the building. The grass smelled so wonderful! The morning air so warm and fresh. I was so thrilled to be outside!

I had to get home.

I had a hunch — and the hunch was right. I spotted my bike, resting against the back wall of the lab, hidden by a large Dumpster.

I leaped onto it and started to pedal. Riding a bike never felt as exciting, so *thrilling*!

I was getting away, away from the horror of crazy Dr. Gray and his freezing lab.

I pedaled faster. I rode without stopping. Without *seeing*! The world was a blur of green.

I must have set a speed record for getting home.

I roared up the driveway, the tires sending gravel flying on both sides.

Then I jumped off my bike and let it topple to the grass. I dove for the kitchen door and burst into the kitchen. "Mom!" I cried.

She jumped up from the breakfast table. I caught the worried expression on her face. It melted away as I ran into the room.

"Dana!" she cried. "Where *were* you? We've all been so terrified. The police are looking for you and — and — "

"I'm okay!" I told her. I gave her a quick hug.

Dad ran in from the hallway. "Dana — you're okay? Where *were* you all night? Your mother and I — "

"Egg monsters!" I cried. "Egg monsters from Mars! Hurry!" I grabbed Dad's hand and tugged. "Come on!"

"Huh?" Dad spun around. He narrowed his eyes, studying me. "What did you say?"

"No time to explain!" I gasped. "They've got Dr. Gray. He's evil, Dad. He's so evil!"

"Who has *what*?" Mom demanded.

"The egg creatures! From Mars! Hurry! There's no time!"

They didn't move. I saw them exchange glances.

Mom stepped forward and placed a hand on my forehead. "Do you have a fever, Dana? Are you sick?"

"No!" I screamed. "Listen to me! Egg creatures from Mars! Follow me!"

I know I wasn't explaining myself too well. But I was frantic.

"Dana — come lie down," Mom instructed. "I'll call Dr. Martin."

"No — please! I don't need a doctor!" I protested. "Just follow me — okay? You've got to see them. You've got to see the egg creatures. You've got to hurry."

Mom and Dad exchanged worried glances again.

"I'm not crazy!" I shrieked. "I want you to come with me to the science lab!"

"Okay, okay," Dad finally agreed. "You were in that lab last night?"

"Yes," I told him, shoving him to the kitchen door. "I called and called. But you couldn't hear me."

"Oh, wow," Dad murmured, shaking his head. "Wow."

The three of us climbed into the car.

It took about three minutes to drive to the lab. Dad parked in front. I jumped out of the car before he stopped.

The front door to the lab stood wide open, as I'd left it.

I ran inside with Mom and Dad close behind me.

"They're egg creatures," I told them breathlessly. "They dropped down from Mars. They captured Dr. Gray."

I led the way down the long hall.

I pushed open the door to the freezing back room.

Mom and Dad stepped in behind me.

I gazed around the room — and gasped in amazement!

32

I saw Mom and Dad staring at me. They had worried expressions on their faces.

"Where are the egg creatures?" Mom demanded softly.

Dad rested a hand gently on my shoulder. "Where are they, Dana?" he asked in a whisper.

"Uh . . . they're gone," I choked out.

The lab stood empty.

No Dr. Gray. No egg creatures. No one.

Bare white walls. Nothing on the floor.

Nothing.

"Maybe they went back to Mars," I murmured, shaking my head.

"And Dr. Gray? What about Dr. Gray?" Dad asked.

"Maybe they took Dr. Gray with them," I replied.

"Let's go home," Mom sighed. "Let's get you into bed, Dana."

Dad guided me from the room, his hands on my

shoulders. "I'll call Dr. Martin," he said softly. "I'm sure we can get him to come to the house this morning."

"I — I do feel a little strange," I admitted.

So they drove me home and tucked me into bed.

The doctor came later that morning and examined me. He didn't find anything wrong. But he said I should stay in bed and rest for a while.

I knew that Mom and Dad didn't believe my story. I felt bad about that. But I didn't know how to convince them I was telling the truth.

I did feel a little weird.

Just tired, I guess.

I dozed off and woke up and dozed off again.

In the afternoon, I woke up to hear my sister Brandy talking to some friends outside my room. "Dana totally freaked out," I heard Brandy say. "He says he was kidnapped by egg monsters from Mars."

I heard Brandy's friends giggling.

Oh great, I thought bitterly. Now everyone thinks I'm a nut case.

I wanted to call Brandy into my room and tell her what really happened. I wanted to make her believe me. I wanted to make *someone* believe me.

But how?

I fell asleep again.

I was awakened by a voice calling my name. I sat up in bed. The voice floated in from my open bedroom window.

I climbed out of bed and made my way to the window. Anne was calling me from the driveway. "Dana — are you okay? Do you want to come over? I got a new CD-ROM version of *Battle Chess*."

"Cool!" I called down to Anne. "I'll be right over."

I pulled on a T-shirt and a pair of jeans. I was feeling pretty good. Rested. Like my old self.

So happy that everything was back to normal.

I hummed to myself as I brushed my hair. I stared at myself in the mirror.

You had an amazing adventure, Dana, I told myself. Imagine — you spent a night with egg creatures from Mars!

But now you're okay, and your life is back to normal.

I felt so happy, I gave Brandy a hug on my way down the stairs. She stared at me as if I truly were crazy!

Humming loudly, I made my way out the kitchen door and started across the yard to Anne's house.

Everything looked so beautiful to me. The grass. The trees. The spring flowers. The sun setting behind the trees.

What a day! What a beautiful, perfect, normal day!

And then halfway across Anne's lawn, I stopped.

I crouched down on the grass — and I laid the biggest egg you ever saw!

About the Author

R.L. STINE is the author of over three dozen best-selling thrillers and mysteries for young people. Recent titles for teenagers include *I Saw You That Night!*, *Call Waiting*, *Halloween Night II*, *The Dead Girlfriend*, and *The Baby-sitter IV*, all published by Scholastic. He is also the author of the *Fear Street* series.

Bob lives in New York City with his wife, Jane, and fifteen-year-old son, Matt.

Add *more*

Goosebumps®

to your collection . . .
A chilling preview of
what's next from
R.L. STINE

THE BEAST FROM THE EAST

2

"What do you want to do?" Nat demanded. He had picked up a thin tree branch to use as a walking stick. Pat kept slapping at it, trying to make Nat stumble.

We had followed the stream for a while. I saw a million tiny, silver minnows swimming near the surface. Now we were making our own path through the tangle of trees, low shrubs, and rocks.

"Hide-and-seek!" Pat declared. He slapped Nat. "You're It!"

Nat slapped him back. "You're It."

"You're It!"

"You're It!"

"You're It!"

The slaps kept getting harder.

"I'll be It!" I cried. Anything to keep them from murdering each other. "Hurry. Go hide. But don't go too far."

I leaned against a tree, shut my eyes, and

started to count to one hundred. I could hear them scampering into the trees.

After thirty, I counted by tens. I didn't want to give them too big a head start. "Ready or not, here I come!" I called.

I found Pat after only a few minutes. He had crouched behind a large white mound of sand. He thought he was hidden. But I spotted his brown hair poking up over the top of the sand.

I tagged him easily.

Nat was harder to find. He had climbed a tree, of course. He was way up at the top, completely hidden by thick clumps of green leaves.

I never would have found him if he hadn't spit on me.

"Get down, creep!" I shouted angrily. I waved a fist up at him. "You're disgusting! Get down — right now!"

He giggled and peered down at me. "Did I hit you?"

I didn't answer. I waited for him to climb down to the ground. Then I rubbed a handful of dried leaves in his face until he was sputtering and choking.

Just a typical Wald family hide-and-seek game.

After that, we chased a squirrel through the woods. The poor thing kept glancing back at us as if he didn't believe we were chasing after him. He finally got tired of the race and scurried up a tall pine tree.

I glanced around. The trees in this part of the woods grew close together. Their leaves blocked most of the sunlight. The air felt cooler here. In their shade, it was nearly as dark as evening.

"Let's go back," I suggested. "Mom and Dad might be getting worried."

The boys didn't argue. "Which way?" Nat asked.

I glanced around, making a complete circle with my eyes. "Uh . . . that way." I pointed. I was guessing. But I felt ninety-nine percent sure.

"Are you sure?" Pat asked. He eyed me suspiciously. I could see he was a little worried. Pat didn't like the outdoors as much as Nat and me.

"Sure I'm sure," I told him.

I led the way. They followed close behind. They had both picked up walking sticks. After we had walked a few minutes, they started fighting a duel with them.

I ignored them. I had my own worries. I wasn't sure we were walking in the right direction. In fact, I felt totally turned around.

"Hey — there's the stream!" I cried happily.

I immediately felt better. We weren't lost. I had picked the right direction.

Now all we had to do was follow the stream back to the clearing where we had set up camp.

I began to hum again. The boys tossed their sticks into the stream. We began to jog along the grassy shore.

"Whoa!" I cried out when my left boot started to sink. I nearly fell into a deep mud patch. I pulled my hiking boot up. Soaked in wet, brown mud up over the ankle.

Pat and Nat thought that was a riot. They laughed and slapped each other high fives.

I growled at them, but I didn't waste any words. They're both hopeless. So totally immature.

Now I couldn't wait to get back to camp and clean the thick mud off my boot. We jogged along the shore, then cut through the skinny, white-trunked trees and into the clearing.

"Mom! Dad!" I called, hurrying over the grass. "We're back!"

I stopped so short, both boys tumbled into me.

My eyes searched the clearing.

"Mom? Dad?"

They were gone.

3

"They left us!" Pat exclaimed. He ran frantically around the clearing. "Mom! Dad!"

"Earth to Pat," Nat called. He waved his hand in front of Pat's face. "We're in the wrong place, you wimp."

"Nat is right," I replied, glancing around. There were no footprints, no tent markers. We were in a different clearing.

"I thought you knew the way, Ginger," Pat complained. "Didn't they teach you anything at that nature camp?"

Nature camp! Last summer my parents forced me to spend two weeks at an "Explore the Great Outdoors" camp. I got poison ivy the first day. After that, I didn't listen to anything the counselors said.

Now I wished I had.

"We should have left markers on the trees," I said, "to find our way back."

"*Now* you think of it?" Nat groaned, rolling his

eyes. He picked up a long, crooked stick and waved it in my face.

"Give me that," I ordered.

Nat handed me the stick. Yellow sap oozed onto my palm. It smelled sour.

"Gross!" I shouted. I tossed the stick away. I rubbed my hands on my jeans. But the yellow stain wouldn't come off my palm.

That's weird, I thought. I wondered what the stuff was. I definitely didn't like it on my skin.

"Let's follow the stream," I suggested. "Mom and Dad can't be too far."

I tried to sound calm. But I was totally twisted around. In fact, I had no idea where we were.

We headed out of the clearing and back to the shore. The sun fell lower in the sky. It prickled the back of my neck.

Pat and Nat tossed pebbles into the water. After a few minutes, they tossed them at each other.

I ignored them. At least they weren't throwing anything at me.

As we walked along, the air became cooler. The path grew narrower.

The water turned dark and murky. Silvery-blue fish snapped at the air. The skinny branches of the tall trees reached down toward us.

A feeling of dread swept over me. Nat and Pat grew quiet. They actually stopped picking on each other.

"I don't remember any of these bushes near our campsite," Pat said nervously. He pointed to a short, squat plant. Its strange blue leaves looked like open umbrellas stacked one on top of the other. "Are you sure we're going the right way?"

By now I was sure we *weren't* headed in the right direction. I didn't remember those strange bushes, either.

Then we heard a noise on the other side of the shrubs.

"Maybe that's Mom and Dad!" Pat exclaimed.

We pushed our way through the plants. And ran into another *deserted* clearing.

I glanced around. This grassy field was enormous. Large enough for a hundred tents.

My heart hammered against my chest.

We stood on rust-colored grass. It stuck up over my ankle. A clump of gigantic purple cabbage plants grew to our right.

"This place is cool!" Nat cried. "Everything is so big."

To me, the clearing wasn't cool at all. It gave me the creeps.

Strange trees surrounded us on all sides. Their branches shot out at right angles to the trunk. They resembled stairs going up and up and up. Up into the clouds.

They were the tallest trees I'd ever seen. And perfect for climbing.

Red moss clung to the branches. Yellow gourds hung from braided vines, swaying in the air.

Where were we? This looked like a weird jungle — not the woods! Why were all the trees and plants so strange?

A knot formed in the pit of my stomach.

Where was our clearing? Where were Mom and Dad?

Nat jogged over to a tree. "I'm climbing up," he said.

"No, you don't," I protested. I rushed over and pulled his arm from the branch.

The red moss rubbed against my palm. My skin turned red where I touched it. Now I had a yellow-and-red design on my hand.

What's going on here? I wondered.

Before I could show my hand to my brothers, the tree started to shake.

"Whoa! Watch out!" I cried.

A small furry animal jumped out of the branches and landed at my feet. I had never seen anything like it before. It was the size of a chipmunk, brown all over except for a white patch around one eye.

It had a bushy tail and floppy ears like a bunny. And two big front teeth like a beaver. Its flat nose twitched. It stared at me with gray eyes, round with fear. I watched it scurry away.

"What was that?" Pat asked.

I shrugged. I wondered what other kinds of weird creatures lived in these woods.

"I'm kind of scared," Pat admitted, huddling close to me.

I felt scared too. But I knew I was the big sister. So I told him everything was okay.

Then I glanced down. "Nat! Pat!" I shouted. "Look!"

My muddy boot stood inside a footprint three times the size of mine. No — even bigger. What kind of animal had a footprint that huge?

A bear? A giant gorilla?

I didn't have time to think about it.

The ground started to tremble.

"Do you feel that?" I asked my brothers.

"It's Dad!" Pat shouted.

It definitely was not Dad. He's a big guy. But no way could he make the ground shake that way!

I heard grumbles and growls from somewhere in the distance. And then a roar. Twigs and branches snapped loudly in the air.

All three of us gasped as a tall beast stomped through the trees. It was huge. So tall that its head touched the middle branches.

It had a narrow, pointy head over a long neck. Its eyes shone like bright green marbles. Shaggy blue fur covered every part of its body. Its long, furry tail thumped heavily on the ground.

The weirdest creature I'd ever seen in my life!

The beast entered the far side of the clearing.

I sucked in my breath as it drew closer. Close

enough for me to see its long snout. Its nostrils flared in and out as it sniffed the air.

My brothers hung back, hiding behind me. We huddled together. Trembling.

The beast opened its mouth. Two rows of sharp, yellow teeth rose up from purple gums. One long, jagged fang slid down over the creature's chin.

I crouched on my hands and knees. Pulled my brothers down with me.

The beast spun around in circles. It sniffed the air and wiggled its hairy, pointed ears. Had it smelled us? Was it searching for us?

I couldn't think. I couldn't move.

The beast turned its ugly head. It stared at me. It saw me.

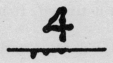

4

My eyes on the creature, I grabbed my brothers by their T-shirts. I dragged them behind some of the huge cabbage plants.

The beast stayed on the other side of the clearing, sniffing the air. It stomped back and forth, sniffing hard. The ground seemed to shake each time one of its furry paws hit the ground. I could feel Nat and Pat shiver with fear.

The beast turned away from us.

Whew! I thought. It hasn't seen us. I bit my bottom lip and held onto Pat and Nat.

"*Argggh,*" the beast grunted. It dropped to all fours. It pressed its snout to the ground and crept along, making loud snuffling noises.

I didn't tell Pat or Nat what I was thinking. The beast hadn't seen us — but there was no way we could keep it from smelling us.

Its long tail swished back and forth. The tail banged against the trees. Gourds fell to the ground.

The beast crawled into the center of the clearing. Closer.

I dug my fingernails into my palm.

Turn around, beast, I prayed. Go back into the woods. The blue creature stopped. It sniffed again. And then it turned. It began to creep in our direction.

I swallowed. Hard. My mouth suddenly felt so dry.

The creature's tail pushed against one of the cabbage plants near us. The leaves rustled.

"Get down!" I whispered, shoving my brothers. We stretched out flat on the ground.

The beast stopped a few feet from our hiding place.

Its tail brushed my arm. The fur felt rough and scratchy.

I jerked my arm away. Could he feel me? Was I like a tiny animal to him? One he could pick up and squeeze the way my brothers teased our dog?

The beast rose up on its hind legs and sniffed. It towered over the cabbage plant. It had to be at least eight feet tall!

It picked at its fur with a clawed thumb — and placed whatever it found in his mouth.

A pleased grin formed under its twitching snout. It peered around the clearing.

Don't look down, I prayed. Don't see us.

My body tensed.

The creature growled and ran its long tongue

over its fang. Then it tromped off into the trees.

I let out a sigh of relief.

"We'd better wait a few minutes," I told my brothers. I counted to one hundred. Then I crawled out from behind the plant. No sign of the creature.

But then I felt the earth shake.

"Oh, no!" I gasped. "Here it comes again!"

Every Beast for Himself!

Goosebumps®

Ginger Wald and her identical twin
brothers, Nat and Pat, are lost in the
woods...and there's something odd going on.
The grass is yellow, the bushes are purple,
and the trees are like skyscrapers.
Then Ginger and her brothers meet
the beasts... big blue furry creatures
who want to play a game.
The winners get to live.
The losers get eaten....

The Beast from the East

Goosebumps #43
by R.L. Stine

Creeping into a bookstore near you!

GET
Goosebumps®
by R.L. Stine

Scare me, thrill me, mail me GOOSEBUMPS now!

Available wherever you buy books, or use this order form. Scholastic Inc., P.O. Box 7502,
2931 East McCarty Street, Jefferson City, MO 65102

Please send me the books I have checked above. I am enclosing $_____ (please add
$2.00 to cover shipping and handling). Send check or money order — no cash or C.O.D.s please.

Name _____ Age _____

Address _____

City _____ State/Zip _____

Please allow four to six weeks for delivery. Offer good in the U.S. only. Sorry, mail orders are not available to
residents of Canada. Prices subject to change.

GB995

Need to send a creepy card?

Boo, dudes! Get ready for a collection of the coolest cards you've ever seen! I have **30** postcards in my all-new Goosebumps® Postcard Book — and each one has a different Goosebumps cover on the front!

Collect 'em, swap 'em, or send 'em to your favorite monster.

Yours ghoully,
Curly

TO:

The
Goosebumps®
Postcard Book

Coming to a bookstore near you.